Wicked Games

SIX10
PUBLISHING

This edition published in 2014 by
Six10 Publishing Limited
11 Deyne Avenue
Prestwich,
Manchester M25 1EJ.
www.six10publishing.co.uk

A catalogue record for this book is available from the British Library.

ISBN: 978-0-9930151-0-6

Lyrics for a Wicked Game: ISAAK, CHRIS © Warner/Chappell Music, Inc.

Wicked Games

Andrew Field

World Was On Fire. No One Could Save Me But You!

1: CHINA

China runs and she runs and she runs, a lung-busting pace to quell the anxiety and the rage that reside permanently inside her. Long strides gobble up exhausting five minute thirty second miles. She pushes herself, punishing her body and distracting her mind before her guests enter Candy's World. If she is running she isn't thinking.

They are waiting while she runs and she runs and she runs. Two wet and cold men huddled outside her front door. They are an hour twenty late. Chip won't be a happy bunny with them messing up his scheduling. She's not a happy bunny either, never has been.

Their knocking is drowned out by Mott the Hoople's Ian Hunter, spitting out the venomous lyrics to The Moon Upstairs, how he hated them and they hated him and he hated everything. She hates her life too, except for Rose. Running stops her bashing herself senseless on Candy's World's white marble floor.

She's been alternatively running and pole dancing ever since Karl and Jenny Grant took Rose to Paradise Hills. Karl, the younger brother of the twins, psychopathic Ged and dumb semi-autistic Denzil, blocking her path. Telling her he'd bring Rose back soon as her guests were gone. No problem. Swear on his life. Dead honest. Don't fret. She's just a mile and a bit down the road, not like she's the other side of the city or anything like that. Call room 203 anytime you want to say hello. Nobody will mind, said Karl on the front step. Wrong rat boy. China minds, big time.

Her daughter's place is by her side, at all times, no exceptions.

China rarely lets Rose stray too far.

When Rose is at primary school, China is in the nearby playground whatever the weather, reading relentlessly and exercising religiously opposite the school. She shadow boxes. Pole dances on climbing frames and slides built for children. Stretches up to the skies, reaching for dark matter's unseen gravitational pull to stabilise her existence. Every now and then she closes her eyes, shuts out the world, feels the summer breeze or the winter's chill on her face, tries to pick out individual sounds of a discordant city in full flow. Mindfulness distracts the scary thoughts pinging unchecked around her head. People laugh, like they do, at her odd antics, her over protective, obsessive nature.

If only they knew.

Her own mother deserted her when she was a couple of years older than Rose is now, returned to her folks across the Atlantic in an airtight wooden box. She was not about to do the same to her daughter. Perhaps…if she momentarily closes her eyes and cannot hear or see her guests knock, may be, just may be, they are not really waiting to be admitted to her world. Unseen and unheard like Berkeley's unobserved philosophical trees falling silently in a forest? The tree question mirrors her own fears and anxieties. Friends, if you can call them that, say it is paranoia. Do they have a point? Just because it happened to her, why should it happen to others? Leopards don't change their spots. Or do they? Expert opinion is, naturally, divided on the matter. She is fully aware that you can always find and twist evidence to justify your argument and build your case, no matter how implausible.

She opens her eyes wide to let in the light and the stark, grim reality of her situation.

Nothing changes, the two men are still waiting, as real as the thin white scars on both her wrists, camouflaged by assorted decorative bangles, hair bands and bracelets.

She slows the treadmill to walking, painfully digs nails into soft palms for extra focus.

She halts the Brain Caper Kids' musical assault on her ears.

Compose yourself bitch. Don't fuck up. Not now, not at the final hurdle. Do whatever they want to get yourself over the finishing line.

I am coming, she shouted, stepping down from the running machine, resisting the urge to distract herself by wrapping her body around the chromium x-pole adjacent to the gym equipment. She removes the chain, undoes the door's deadlocks, drying herself with a towel. Her two unwanted guests bypass her as if she is invisible. Cold air hits her, releasing thousands of butterflies in her stomach. Normally when goat boys catch first sight of her they can barely disguise their transparent desire to download on, or in, her software.

Welcome to Candy's World, she said, plastering a wide cheesecake grin on her face as synthetic as her black lycra leggings and black vest. The stench of excrement overpowers large pans of chilli and bolognese simmering on an Aga. Switchblade Eddie is the culprit, judging by the rear of his stained bulging jeans. The obese shithead normally pokes around the pots in the kitchen or mauls her with short stubby fingers. Today is the exception as he is pawing a bottle of Jack, Lynchburg, Tennessee's finest sour mash whiskey, about to fill a lead crystal tumbler with 40% proof, before deciding to swig direct from the bottle.

You want a slug, catch, said Eddie, hurling the Jack Daniels towards the stranger, who makes no attempt to catch the bottle.

As it smashes the stranger looks at her. She notices ice cold clear blue eyes. China's big on eyes, the windows to the soul if you look deep and hard enough. He glances away, blinks and focuses on Switchblade Eddie.

Drink is the first and last refuge of the gutless, Fat Boy. I'll take that as an offer of a friendly drink rather than an unwise act of aggression, said the stranger, his words overflowing with contempt. Think you need to go home and ask your mummy to change your diapers, you stink.

Wanker, said Eddie, hurling the tumbler to his right, away from them both, hitting a floor-to-ceiling window overlooking the Paradise Hills Resort & Golf Club championship course.

The tumbler shatters, the window stays intact.

China steps back from the firing line. She doesn't want to get hurt in the crossfire. She's seen nasty Switchblade Eddie in action, kicking the unconscious further into unconsciousness long after they've stopped posing any threat.

When you've finished your tantrum Fat Boy close the door behind your shitty arse, said the stranger, one eye on Switchblade, the other on the 24 hour news channel on the television he has just switched on and muted. All three watch the newsflash scrolling across the TV screen: *city centre shooting incident, unconfirmed police reports say at least four people shot dead*. Her stomach churns, the butterflies increase the intensity of their flapping.

She feels an urge to pee.

She's harbouring murderers, that's big time wrist slapping, prison if caught and then Rose is lost forever.

Four, the stranger said softly to himself. Four, the fourth?

Jak, we need to call Chip, said Eddie, his voice strangely polite after his aggressive posturing moments earlier.

You still here, asked Jak.

Got to keep him in the picture, said Eddie.

Can't he watch TV like the rest of us, asked Jak.

He'll be watching more than the television, thinks China, glancing at the huge mirrors that dominate the massive open plan ground floor. Eddie doesn't move or say anything else. She smells his fear alongside the excrement and the chilli and the bolognese. She knows fear's toxic smell, has a PhD in fear herself. Any second the two men will either kick off or the omniscient Chip will intervene. He's always here even when he's not, the tree in the forest reversed. Switchblade Eddie flinches, a mobile ringtone interrupts their staring contest. She answers, knowing who is on the other end. Their physical estrangement does not extend to mobile communications or third party intermediaries.

China, a new wave of nausea sweeps through her, I believe our friends have finally arrived, better late than never I suppose. Entertain them for me, keep them amused in your own inimitable fashion until darkness falls, said Chip.

Shall I fuck them, she asked loudly, too loudly, hooking a thumb in the top of her black lycra leggings, unsure why she's just opened her big gob and shoved her big outsized foot in it. Probably because the bastard has Rose, leaving her impotent, despite their unwritten truce. They may have a pact in place but it is only temporary. Ultimately, she is unable to stop him should he decide to change the rules of engagement.

More words slip out.

Shall I fuck them both? Jak notices her now, Yes Sir, now the 'FUCK' word is given a public airing. Turns from the TV screen, giving her the once over, like she was a second hand motor on its last legs, checking out if he'd get any value out of his hundred quid investment.

He wasn't the first to view her as simple White Trash and won't be the last. She's eyeing him up too, although it's not a fuck buddy she wants. China lusts after a White Stallion Man to rescue her and Rose, A Knight in Shining Armour who is not intimidated by Chip and his tough guy cronies.

No need to be so crude China, I was thinking of a cup of tea, a slice of cake, maybe brunch. No need to overdo the hospitality. You don't want to give it away for free do you, ask Eddie and Jak if their mission was successful, asked Chip. Did they get their man? Will Christian DeVeres be back at work on Monday?

She disguises her shock at the news. A beat. They've murdered dear old porky Chris, a little piggy who could not hurt a fly if you saw him from a distance. Another beat. She manages to do as requested without her voice weakening.

Yes, he's toast, said Jak.

She repeats what he said, aware Chip already knows.

Ask them about Jimmy, said Chip.

Jimmy, she repeated, Chip wants to know about Jimmy.

A total fuck up, Jimmy's bloody dead. Saw it with my own eyes. Jesus, Chip. A fucking nightmare. Switchblade Eddie opens the second bottle of Jack, takes a massive swig.

The man lost his head, said Jak, picked the wrong time to go bus hopping, silly bugger.

She relays the message verbatim, hears a snort of derision

from Chip, he couldn't give a toss about Jimmy Doyle's demise. Or the late Christian DeVeres, no longer blustering in his high pitched voice in Candy's World's kitchen while he cooked the books and cleaned dirty money, no longer smiling his crooked little smile while Rose played, danced and skipped.

The madness moment had finally arrived.

Chip was finally slaughtering his own thinks China. He was ranting at her. Pay attention. No more cock ups. No more deviations. You stick to the plan. Both of you stay put until we come and get you. No calls. No contact with anyone. Radio silence at all times. Understand China? You're responsible for them two. Tell them and get their approval.

She does as she's told on automatic pilot, trying to get her head around the slaughter.

They nod imperceptibly, re-engaging in their tough guy macho staring contest.

I've got to go China, fucking them might be a good idea, stop them killing each other. Better still, let them fight, save us all a lot of bother. Is he watching on his tablet or his phone, thinks China. Is Jenny babysitting Rose or has he already reintroduced himself to her? Rose will be scared if he has, she doesn't welcome strangers. China's taught her to be wary of unknown men.

You two better behave if you want to chill out in Candy's World, or I'll have to give you both a spanking like naughty little boys.

They ignore her, the two of them less than a dozen paces apart. Can she break them up? No chance. Not now Eddie's produced his blade, eight long inches of deadly Sheffield cold steel, clasped tightly in his right hand.

Jak looks and sounds non-plussed.

You as good at maths as your brother was at riding a

motorcycle Fat Boy? How's your memory? What happened to the shooter? Did I drop it when I came off the bike? Did you pick it up? Jak spits out the words with the same ferocity as Ian Hunter spat out his lyrics earlier. You going to play with your little toy knife or whistle Dixie while you tug on your tiny pecker, asked Jak, slowly taking off his soaking jacket, peeling off his black t-shirt, giving Eddie every chance to attack. Jak pulls off black boots, unbuttons 501 black jeans, stands there almost naked in CK boxers, the left side of his body badly grazed. These will need washing and drying once ShitForBrains has fucked off. Can you count Fat Boy? How many left? How fast are you Eddie? Faster than a Black Talon bullet, Fat Boy? Eddie is backing off towards the door, away from Jak.

Chip says stay put.

You, Jak, whatever, you're called, calm down, said China.

Despite herself, she had to agree staying put was better than going back out on to the streets where anything could happen. If they had Jimmy, you didn't have to be a rocket scientist to put Switchblade Eddie Doyle in the frame. Chip said stay. I heard him. Loud and clear. She doesn't want to deal with a vengeful Chip. Isn't it better if he stays? Safer for all of us. If he gets caught he could lead..?

Open the door for him. Leave the toy knife on your way out, said Jak, watching Switchblade Eddie take yet another pull of JD.

She's not moved to the door. Unsure how it's about to play out, unable to take sides in case the other wins.

Put the knife away Lard, unless your slut of a mum wants a two-for-one deal when she buries you and your brother in the same bloody stinking hole, said Jak, who looks younger than Eddie in China's eyes in his boxers and white socks, pure loose limbed grazed prime meat.

A single loud sob from Eddie breaks the tension. Tears,

snot and ming mingle in one gooey mess on his fat blotchy unshaven face.

Bizarrely, China actually feels sorry for him, if sorrow and hatred can be complementary emotions, like anxiety and fear.

She doesn't know.

She is an emotional cripple herself. Only Rose, her only sole priority, keeps her sane. Everything else is lost in the cuckoo's nest. Everything else is propaganda to nick a phrase from a black and white film she'd once watched. Those prophetic lines at the beginning of the movie struck a chord even if the rest bypassed her. She had no time for drunks, self-pity or womanisers.

You're not having my blade you cunt, said Eddie, closing the knife and returning it to his pocket, bristling with indignation despite his broken spirit, backing down from a fight with a defiant whimper.

Jak's intensity reduced him to tears.

Was Armageddon burning behind the ice cold blue eyes? Eddie places the bottle on the work surface, backs off further, looks at her full of grief.

She opens the door for him.

He glides back out into the cold and the wet. She slams the door shut.

China looks over at Jak to see what happens next. She's searching for the words to make the right impression.

He takes the decision away from her, points to his dirty laundry, pulls out a pistol from his jacket.

Sorry about all that. One bullet left. We only had five. He made the right choice. Put my clothes in the wash. Now about this fuck?

2: CHIP

The young girl has more potential than all the other children combined, a skinny strawberry blonde with freckles, a natural elastic swing and a cool temperament to match.

How old is she, Chip asked Rob Dean, his senior golf pro at the Chip Mackie Paradise Hills Golf Academy. He moves towards the child before Rob can answer, playing to his audience of young golfers, parents, a prominent broadsheet journalist, her photographer and an expensive PR consultant he is part funding.

What's your name Sweetie, Chip asked.

Amy, she replied, holding out her right hand for Chip to shake.

How old are you Amy, continued Chip.

Seven, said Amy, confidently and with obvious pride.

Just the right age, thought Chip. Catch them when they're young was his motto.

Soon Rose should be ready for serious lessons as well. He glances towards Play World, where dumb Jenny Grant was babysitting the child in the resort's indoor playground. China was obstinate, playing her silly self-imposed estrangement card for all it was worth. Meant he hardly knew the child, only seen her from a distance these last few years. How could he determine her potential with such limited access? If she could match half of China's promise he would be backing a winner. The upside to the whole *Chris DeVeres fiasco* was it brought one of his major challenges out into the open. They could stop playing games and sidestepping each other, determine he was number one in every respect, the leader of the pack, top dog. Once that was acknowledged they could reconcile and get on with their bloody lives.

Take your stance, he said, kneeling down in front of Amy, feeling the warm glow emanating from her proud parents.

The six-time tour champion and Open runner up Chip Mackie singling out their daughter for special attention. Individual tuition from an acknowledged Master Golfer.

They are chuffed their Amy is going to be photographed by the national press.

He winks at the journalist and PR. Flashes them a big smile to show them they are both very much on his mind, despite or because of the clear age gap.

He'd wined and dined the two with Bing, his Paradise Hills business partner, last night. They'd all got a little too high, them more than him. He only ever lets himself go with his Merry Men.

Chip checks out Amy's grip, positions her hands around the shaft until he's happy with the way she's holding it. Most important to get the grip right, he said. Firm. Not too firm. No way you can control the club head if it's not grasped properly. Everything gets sprayed everywhere. Got to avoid deviation at all costs, otherwise it's like watching the Red

Arrows, balls flying in all directions. Everyone laughs. John the photographer clicks away, sweating despite the cold. Chip had seen his prodigious intake last night and was surprised he'd made it out of bed: Ged Grant had a hedonistic rival.

Chip knows his golf audience inside out, easily seduced by celebrity. Journalists, equally gullible, inhabited two camps. Shock jocks high on extreme death/blame tragedies and puff monkeys, writing uncritical pieces, manipulated, flattered and badgered by smart PR girls like Sally Bailey. Journalist Anna Judd fell into the second category. The timing for an upmarket broadsheet profile could not have been better. More witnesses to testify he was an ordinary average guy blessed with a Cartier golf swing and a gritty determination to overcome adversity.

Three things about the swing. Always lock your standing leg and your knee, he said, holding her firmly. Next, rotate your hips and shoulders in unison. That's where your power comes from although don't forget to hit the ball flush too. Do the first part of your swing for me Sweetie, the backwards bit.

Amy does as requested and Chip, now looking at her parents, demonstrates the amount of movement needed for the perfect swing, first rotating her hips, then her shoulders with his hands, still kneeling in front of her. Fingers outlining to her parents the various muscle groups necessary to power the swing.

These generate the extra yards that will one day win Amy championships, said Chip. You saw her here first Anna. Snap away John buddy, these pics are your pension plan. Chip always encourages his Merry Men to think of revenue opportunities.

In his peripheral vision he sees his business partner talking to a slime ball. Beyond them, a motorcade of half a dozen expensive luxury cars. The Khans, Tommy and Bobby, arriving for an Asian wedding and to collect special golf merchandise. They run a successful international fast fashion business and never need to work again. But like him, they love the challenge of business. Love it despite the stress. Tommy almost died of a heart attack a while back but, full of pills and a low carb diet, bounced back for more. Their latest venture involved online golf merchandise, specifically bulk buying balls, a clever risk-free trick Chip and Ged had developed, an alternative way to fund the resort's current cash shortfall.

Perfect, the final tip is to stick your butt out just so. That way your body shape can really get in position to give those balls a right thwack, he said, standing behind Amy, bending her slightly forward, positioning her with gentle, soft hands. Go on hit a few Sweetie, show us what you can do, he said, adjusting his clothing before joining the girl's parents.

There are two dozen kids participating in the introductory weekend academy session for new junior golfing talent. Amy is the only girl of note. Long term, she's worth several thousand in tuition fees and a lot more to Chip if she stays hooked and ambitious.

She looks really good, Chip announced to the crowd. Easily makes the grade with the right coaching and mentoring. Great shot sweetie. A born natural. Better than I was at that age. Course, I soon got the hang of it. Anybody want to see, he asked, smiling as his audience cried out an excited yes as one. Driver Rob, requested Chip. His golf pro throws a club to Chip, who catches and twirls the metal stick, a drum major showboating as he leads a ticker tape victory parade. Golf was showbiz, just like anything else that generated cash. OK make way for the Mighty 'Chip' Mackie, let us see if I've still got the juice, not hit a ball in anger for ages and I am getting on a bit, mid forties you know, not sure the old bones are up to the challenge, old ticker not in the best of shape. In my prime, when I had more hair and less paunch, I could hammer a ball 350 yards no problem. One golf writer said I had a swing that would break the back of an ordinary mortal, let's see if I've still got it, shall we, asked Chip. The same writer had said Chip had rabbit ears under pressure. Him and Ged had left him with cauliflower ones late at night after a skinful, ambushed him in a golf club car park. The writer never dissed Chip Mackie in print or looked him in the face again. Chip places the ball on the tee, takes a few clumsy practice swings. Swish. Swish. Swish. Bit rusty, he said to general laughter, his audience expectant and excited. Let's make this the Big One, Ready, Steady, Let's Go Big with the White Bullets, said Chip. The Big Wind Up, club head thrust so far back it is digging into the back of his powerful, muscular legs. The huge surge decelerates once the club head passes his head. When he hits the ball it grasshops a hundred yards. Nobody saw that coming after the Huge Wind Up. Damn, timing is AWOL, said Chip. Always make people laugh. You could not go far wrong. Think I need another go, shall I have another go, he asked. His audience aren't really fooled, they know what he's going to do next and are sharing the post modern ironic joke. I'll pretend I am bad and then show you I'm not.

Chip separates six brand new balls from the pile, lines them up in a row, not bothering with tees. Feels the buzz of excitement rise.

He likes that.

Looks at Anna and Sally. Winks at them. They wink back. Connecting.

He likes that too. Chip connects.

He's a people person. That's what he told the journalist the previous night while they devoured fresh lobsters the size of canoes.

Planning is key. Planning and preparation.

Never deviate from your chosen path. Under any circumstances. I always visualise my shot, play it over and over in my head like I am in a Hollywood blockbuster where I am the Big Star. I am executing the perfect shot each time. I know I'll get the perfect result if I put all the appropriate knowledge stored in my head behind that shot. When I line up on the first tee of a Big Comp I visualise the Big Trophy at the end with the equally Big Cheque after completing 72 holes with the lowest score. Like I did when I won the China Open. In Spain twice. Scotland twice. Portugal, once, said Chip, looking at Amy's parents and all the other mums and dads wanting to fulfil their own lost dreams and missed opportunities through their children. Winks at them all. Connecting with them all. He's a people person rebuffing a migraine that wants to settle in for an impromptu long-stay vacation. He feels good after the shockwaves of a truly horrific last 24 hours. Harry Wade's call saying Christian DeVeres had gone rogue. Chip visualised Chris's demise and arranged it pronto before any damage could be inflicted by the weak bastard's promiscuous Big Mouth. His visualisation excluded Ged and Denzil Grant because they were collecting golf balls. He visualised a clean execution, not today's carnage. The planning had gone awry. The escape cumbersome. Still, he'd get it sorted. While others procrastinated, Chip Mackie acted fast. Created new plans. Making a mistake once was bad luck, repeating the same error was sheer stupidity.

I am picturing these six balls sailing way beyond the walls of this driving range, you guys watching, asked Chip. The swing should be effortless, all timing and co-ordination, swish. He visualised DeVeres' fat bespectacled balding head as the ball. The club hits its square. The ball takes offenders on a really low trajectory, appearing to defy gravity, soaring high into the overcast sky. Chip feels the awe in the audience as they watch the ball. Visualise and repeat, he said under his breath to himself, repeating the exercise five more times, his body a metronome, tick, tock, tick, tock, tick, Jimmy, Eddie, Bing, Turner's monkey, China. The effort causes a little breathlessness, he winks at Amy, the only one not following the path of the balls.

She looks at him, connecting.

He glances at Play World, Jenny and Rose nowhere to be seen.

He'd told Jenny he wanted Rose to watch. Get her interested.

He'd explained about today being an important stepping stone for the child, except dumb Jenny could not understand simple concepts, like most women. Hair extensions and false nails and enlarged silicone boobs yes, simple instructions, however, were beyond her comprehension.

Time to move on.

He needs to talk to Hugh 'Bing' Bingham, his 'toff' business partner. Love to see you all again when you sign up for the academy sessions. Rob will sort you out. Amy's got the 'golden girl' look, haven't you sweetie? I've got another protege too, old Chip's onto a real winner, said Chip. He waves, she waves back.

He smiles.

She smiles.

Connecting. One big future bonus from the mire. He was looking forward to working with her. And Rose. He could picture Amy and Rose becoming good friends, lifelong friends, a great starting point for them all. He shakes hands with numerous parents, tells the PR girl to ensure Anna gets suitable quotes from the parents and kids while John needs to snap more pictures. He'll join them again in ten, just got to sort out a spot of business.

Bing starts the ball rolling, talking like he's chewing a ping pong ball. His face has that 'happy-stupid-in-love' glaze when he's making hay with a woman who is not his wife. The PR girl is the most likely cause of his puppy-like adoration. Two toffs feeding off each other, the younger posh bint fancying a tilt at a title just in case Bing's wife ever vacates her position. She probably knows Bing could never afford a divorce or had the balls to tell his wife he wanted one, not that the PR girl minded. There was plenty of time to snap up a suitable Handsome Hooray Henry with her inheritance. Let the toffs indulge in their toffary, thought Chip. There was a time and a place for the conch to chat and now was not the time.

Hi Chip, can I introduce...bumbles the peer of the realm.

Chip cuts him short. No need. We've met, unfortunately. I want to chat with Bing if you don't mind, brushing off the *red hot salesman with the self-proclaimed Midas touch* as if he were dandruff on his jacket. We've got your number, bye bye, we'll call you if we're desperate, said Chip.

That was a bit rude and unnecessary old chap, said Bing, once the salesman had gone.

You know who he is, asked Chip.

A property expert who can guarantee selling our lodges at top dollar, said Bing, smiling at his smart find.

His name is Norman Nugent Monk, a convicted fraudster and major league bankrupt. Once worth nearly a billion in his Walter Mitty fantasies. He's an irrelevance to us. To everyone. He's best crawling back under the stone from where he was spawned. We've got more pressing matters. You've got an Asian wedding to look after, said Chip.

Were we successful with the other, ahem, situation, asked Bing.

Depends what you call a 'success'. Your chirpy old bean counter won't be coming back to work anytime soon. In fact, he won't be doing anything anymore on account of having a great big permanent headache caused by a gaping hole in his skull, said Chip.

I've not heard anything, said Bing.

You will do soon enough, going to be headline news for the next 48 hours. One of mine took a tumble. But I've got another chap and Turner's wrecking ball holed up nearby. Your man Turner still OK to extricate as per our plan or do we need an alternative?

Like, asked Bing, nervously picking his immaculate fingernails at Chip's news.

Elimination was Chip's preferred option. Dead men don't dance or grass on friends and employers. The accountant tried, sentenced and executed within 24 hours by a judge and jury of one, Chip. A plan conceived in the time it takes to play a couple of holes of golf.

Not that he would share his opinion with Bing.

The lanky streak had almost pissed himself just now. Despite a gene pool dating back to the middle ages, Bing was weak, like all the toffs who believed they were feudal lords ruling over the peasants.

Chip had their cards marked.

All of them.

Every single last one of the bastards. Tomorrow belonged to him and the Grants, a breed apart, the future, the Merry Men who would make Merry.

Chip calls Ged, can barely hear him above the Stone Roses wanting to be adored.

He pictures the twins, as different as chalk and cheese, side by side in the van, singing to the loud melodic music, pretending they were in their twenties and not two dozen years too old. Denzil hardly ever spoke but loved to sing loudly, how weird was that? They all laughed about their childish ways, mind, could see the daftness in buckets of Ged and Denzil's refusal to grow old gracefully. They weren't called the Merry Men without good cause.

How long, asked Chip. Two hours max, said Ged, yelling above the adoration demanded by Ian Brown, everything OK?

Sure, said Chip, everything is always OK. You bothered listening to the news?

You what, is the Pope Catholic, asked Ged. Laters Bud.

Much as he loved Ged, he was a hothead and did not need to be wound up more than he usually was. Fortunately, current affairs and listening to the radio were not high on his list of priorities. Ged would be annoyed they had used an outsider to wipe out Chris DeVeres. Ged always said things should stay in-house. Chip would talk him round over a wet or two. The other two brothers would always follow their older brother's lead, Karl was a puppy always wanting to please, Denzil intense, never really offered an opinion about anything, there one minute, gone the next. He wasn't sure Denzil was a full shilling, not that he'd mention it to Ged. He was very protective of his younger twin. He'd seen the damage Ged would inflict on anyone foolish enough to rip Denzil, who never seemed offended no matter what anyone said to him. Perhaps he didn't understand.

Chip spots Tommy and Bobby Khan heading towards the hotel reception, the heavyweight businessmen not only had access to cash to buy wholesale cocaine shaped as golf balls but had also hired him the gun and sold him five explosive Black Talon bullets, the best on the market. They were here to collect the coke balls hidden amongst legitimate product. Their cash purchase would give Chip a larger bite of Paradise and keep greedy predator creditors at bay while they waited for sales to pick up.

His migraine eases slightly as he watches Amy's cute swing, Anna and John fussing over her. He had SO wanted to introduce Rose to golf today, although he knew he would have to show a bit more patience, which wasn't really his forte. China was a chip off the old block, if you'd excuse the pun. She was smart, very smart, danced rings around the likes of Jenny and Bing. She'd run rings around him too if he let her, except he was hip to her every move.

He digs into his pocket.

Brings out his mobile. Goes to the live stream.

China and Turner's Monkey, banging away like a couple of rabbits. Makes him feel a bit sick. Delves back into his pockets.

Pops another couple of pain killers from a small blister pack.

Once China had been just as cute as Amy and Rose until she deviated big time. He'd loved her so much and she'd loved him. Gradually, she'd turned for no reason, become distant and withdrawn, swung from adoration to insolence. He'd given her the best he could afford and asked only for unconditional love in return. When her golf had gone to pot, he'd paid for piano lessons, dance lessons, singing lessons, any bloody lessons she wanted to make her happy. He knew the ultimate answer to China's problems. Same as the monarchy. They'd have to skip Big Ears in favour of Young King Bill and Kit Kat Kate. Bing had gone to the wedding, was on the Xmas card list, probably had their mobile numbers. Chip Mackie was never going to be invited to that party of privilege but he would have his own bloody kingdom, his own bloody fiefdom, and it was up to China to decide if she wanted to join the rest of the Merry Men and Merry Women at King Chip's and Princess Rose's court.

3: CHINA

China swipes Eddie from her mind, dumps him unceremoniously in her metaphorical trash bin.

She wants to concentrate on the near-naked White Stallion Man about to ride to her rescue.

Fate. Kismet. Karma. Take your pick. She was evolving her Once-In-A-Lifetime, Two-For-One offer in her head.

She asks if he wants coffee and imagines four human souls travelling faster than the speed of light, chasing stardust amongst the universe's billions of stars and planets. They are heading towards the Southern Pinwheel, no doubt, only a mere 15 million light years away in the constellation Hydra. How mad was that? Tough enough surviving one day at a time without contemplating why a supreme being wants so much bloody room to play his or her insane mind games. No wonder she was an atheist, four dead on a cold wet Sunday morning, as unfathomable as light travelling from the Southern Pinwheel. A fair God would not allow such cruelty perpetrated in his name. She'd read during catastrophes like the Black Plague and the Nazi Holocaust, survivors rejected their gods for not intervening. She agreed with their conclusions from her own experiences. Why would a supreme entity consider it appropriate to allow such suffering and deprivation? As far as she was concerned, humans were skeletons draped in meat and muscle, hitching a ride on a rock spinning across space. One day the entire human race would be destroyed and only space dust would be left, nothing more, nothing less. We'd all be heading towards the Southern Pinwheel.

Concentrate China, concentrate on the White Stallion Man.

She pinches her hand.

Smells the chilli and the bolognese. Mindfulness distracts her inner head chimp from rioting. China said she does instant, filtered or espresso. Machine's crap at the frothy milky ming. Doesn't want to get done by the Office of Fair Trading for fobbing him off with an alleged cappuccino. Her joke falls flat. He's watching the screen. *Four dead*, no more details. Tells him she can rustle up a quick gut fuck, regrets using the f-word instantly. She quickly moves on with the menu options. Full English, the works, sausage, fried eggs, mushrooms, tomatoes, bacon, hash browns, black pudding, baked beans and chips. Scrambled eggs and smoked salmon. Welsh rarebit with a fried egg in the middle, two or three slices like her mum, your mum, might have made you after a few pints. Before she took another way out. She barely knew her. What sort of woman would desert her own child, leaving the poor thing to fend for itself without any explanation or even a goodbye?

Newsflash updates: more details. *Four dead. One a police officer. The second an arrested man who had been in the custody of the police.* She assumed the latter was Chris.

Nothing on the other two. Jimmy Doyle, according to Eddie, was the third. The fourth? China repeats her hostess rap in case he wasn't paying attention on account of slaughtering four people. There's chilli or bolognese if he can wait an hour. She makes pots of both each weekend for a homeless charity in the city.

About the fuck, he asked. No escape. All men are goats, only want to get their ends away, the only language they truly understand. Play the Game, the Wicked Game. Play to his fantasies. She stands in front of him. Hands on hips, expectant without expectation.

China has her own fantasies about escape. A beach in the sun. A little business serving freshly cooked food to tourists and the locals. Europe, possibly Italy or Spain, some place with a decent climate. A simple menu for people who appreciate good unpretentious food. Use only local produce. Pots of chilli and bolognese, lasagne and a dish for the veggies. Once a pot was two thirds empty she'd make another. She didn't want to change the world with her little restaurant by the sea. Two dozen covers, a couple of waiting staff and her and a boyfriend to help her keep it ticking over. Rose would love it. They'd have animals as pets too. Music and laughter would fill her restaurant. Live music late into the night as they danced by candlelight, percussion provided by nearby lapping waves.

That's an unreal dream. A distant dumb fantasy. Cheeky wanting better. The cold stark reality is standing in front of her. What did the song say: *World Was On Fire, No One Could Save Me But You?* Nobody could save me but you Jak, is that true Mr White Stallion Man? She'll play the song if they frolic. Music takes away the banality of casual sex. Slap on the greasepaint and surrender to the ordeal one more time, hoping it doesn't eat you up, send you spiralling into the depths of insanity, chased by mad shadows from here to the Southern Pinwheel and beyond.

Less talk, more action.

Anything for this, asked Jak, CK boxers hitting the deck. She checks out his semi-tumescence, notices his badly grazed body carved out of granite.

You want me to clean you up? Must be really painful, said China.

Afterwards. Anything, he said, glancing down at his growing friend.

She dips into a box on a table and pulls out a strawberry flavour condom and lube. She should be grateful her White Stallion Man's not proposing a bareback ride. China picks up a slimline remote for the Bang Olufsen.

Where, she asked.

Here will do, he replied.

Whatever you do, don't pull my hair, she said, sliding skin tight black lycra leggings down over her hips and thighs. The most important fuck of her life, potentially. He moves behind the settee, motions for her to stand in front of him. Takes the package from her hand and rips.

Going to be pretty rudimentary, he said. You want to grease up the frying pan a bit. Dry's no fun for you or me.

She unscrews the top. Dabs cold jell on hot fingers. *Is Jak her man?* Her free hand grabs him. Works the rod, conscious the noise of the bracelets and trinkets decorating her wrists might put him off. Changes the playlist. From Angry to Amorous. Presses play. Wicked Game. A choice? James Vincent McMorrow's haunting acoustic rendering recorded live in St Canice Cathedral in Kilkenny, Ireland or Chris Isaak's original. The latter won. Just. *World was on Fire. No One Could Save Me. But You.*

Music off, he said.

I love this song. Fuck better with tunes. The music dictates our rhythm, said China.

Off, he repeated.

Play something else for you, what do you like, she asked.

Bloody silence when I am on the job. If I wanted musical chairs I'd have stayed at home and hired some kids for the afternoon, said Jak. Now turn it off and lean forward. Not up for debate.

No argument. She liked that. Liked it a lot. She bent forward. Letting him position her. Strong confident hands getting her as he wanted. She glances at the two tall mirrors nearest her. Keeps her face neutral. Cameras recording the *dirty deed*. You watching Chip? This won't be exciting you will it? We're too old. Jak's still glued to the TV screen as he enters. The talking head jabbering. The news about the shootings unchanged. Four still dead. No names. One cop. One suspect. Nothing on the other two.

They frolic.

Jak watching the TV. China watching him in the mirrors. Feeling him deep inside her. Big Question still unanswered: *was Jak her man?* Time wasn't on her side now. Chip's modus operandi had changed in a single explosive wet Sunday morning in a wet city. Chris DeVeres was dead. Jimmy Doyle was dead. Eddie Doyle was imploding. Rose too close to bad company. Leopards don't change their spots voluntarily. You had to make them. Nothing she could do by herself. She didn't have the strength. She could not watch over Rose forever. She could not fight wild animals without having her own ferocious wild beast. *World Was On Fire. And it was about to get a lot hotter. Only Jak could save them. She'd have one free hit at Chip and his Merry Men of Sociopaths.* Feel good, said China.

It's OK, who's Danny, he asked. Danny? A red, green and blue 'shield' tattoo on her right buttock. *China Loves Danny* in italics underneath. An underaged drunken pier trip, a declaration of undying love, an act of early teen rebellion, a red rag to a wild and furious bull. Her dad? In the mirror he is checking framed photographs of her and Rose that should come down when Candy's World becomes a film studio or a sanctuary for murderers. She had forgotten to hide them in her rage and anxiety. How old?

That awful age. Fast approaching six, she replied.

Very pretty, he said.

Ugly I think. Not very attractive at all. Not very special, she said.

Boost her confidence why not, he said.

How long you planning on taking, she asked. Squeezing him, gyrating her buttocks into his groin to try and hasten proceedings to a quicker conclusion. Hoping he wasn't a harris merchant and would deviate without any warning. She always thought it was straight out bent for blokes inclined that way.

She's not going to burst in, asked Jak.

Child minders, she replied.

On a weekend, he countered.

I was working, she lied. Before you interrupted and entered. She feels fingers searching and successfully finding her button. Unusual, a gentle touch at odds with his aggression. Showed consideration. Care. Sharing. A kind man. Not going about his business like a DIY nutcase sanding wooden floor boards. The talking head gone from the screen. An on-the-spot female reporter talks silently to camera, behind her flashing blue lights illuminate steps and the city's most exclusive hotel. Top left, a grainy CCTV snapshot that could easily be Jak if you knew him. If she could lip read they'd be telling her the man was armed and dangerous and should not be approached under any circumstances.

And here he is.

Deep inside her.

You going to take all day, she asked. Conscious of their bizarre coupling. The two of them locked together as one. Chatting away as if they were having a coffee and bite to eat in a cafe, not fucking. She feels him pulling on her hair. Wanting to ride her like a horse. He knows the score. She knows the score. After she'd asked him so fucking politely. He's watched too many porno movies. Like Switchblade Eddie and all the other lowlife scumbags thinking jizz on the face was what a girl wanted dripping off her chin after the dust was puffed.

A sharp elbow drives hard into his ribs.

Hurts her, hurts him more.

He grunts. Leave my fucking hair ShitHead, she said. His rhythm interrupted.

They almost tumble. Balance lost. He slips out and is back in again, grasping hips. She's turned the music back on. *World was on Fire*. His ribs better be.

Sorry, he said. An apologetic assassin. No longer fussing about the music. The slide guitar relaxed her. Eased the tension as her heartbeat twice as fast as the Wicked Game. You going to deliver your load or carry on whistling bloody Dixie, she said, pleased with her witty repetition. Takes his line and uses it as her own. Clever China. She feels his body tighten and jerk as the TV screen reveals the other two dead: *one of the perpetrators and a four year old boy caught in the crossfire.*

Four years of age, he whispered.

The child's age didn't interfere with Jak's performance. She'd never understand men. Not even if she lived to be a million. They were wired differently to women that was for sure. They could kill and fuck and feel nothing. Women had evolved while men still inhabited caves.

4: JAK

A four year old child?

The news comes on screen the same time as he comes inside the girl.

He buckles, holds her torso tight, spent, replays the execution.

Action review: he'd fired four shots, entered the op light on ammunition and light on every other front. Fired two rounds during the first contact. They had come in at the wrong angle, the error cost vital seconds, forced them to pull up face on rather than sideways. The lapse had given the mark's escort reaction time, a woman in a black leather jacket between him and the target. He had blasted her to get to him, caught her in the front of her skull. He reasoned it would pass through her and enter the target. The second a direct hit between the eyes of the man Eddie Doyle had identified moments before. He fired two more into the chest as the intended victim fell to the ground. The child must have been hit by one of those bullets after they had passed through the man's body, the only way it could have happened.

Action review alternative take: look for alternatives, anywhere else? Jimmy, like his brother, had crapped himself, sped off far too quickly when there was no need to panic. If they'd rehearsed and planned the operation, they'd have seen how simple it was to escape safely while everyone was too shocked to react. Instead the bike and Jimmy were under the bus and Jak was rolling, hoping terrified car drivers would slam on screeching brakes in a timely fashion. No child was involved in the initial fatal escape so it had to be the third or fourth bullets, a four year old child killed in the crossfire. Why didn't they listen? His original plan flying into the city was for a long range sniper attack. There was no rush in his view, 48 hours, maybe double that for observation, ID the best place to attack with the least collateral damage and the best escape. He'd explained all that to Chip in the car park overlooking the moors and the customer had just shook his head. Trebled his money on the spot, told him today, had to be today. Like the fool he was, Jak said yes and now a small child was shot stone dead.

Jak had been involved in killing young children before, the last time caused major meltdown, Post Traumatic Stress Disorder according to Turner at Alex's funeral.

Jak had held it together until the burial, not sure what tipped him over. All the pomp and circumstance, the ceremonial. His country's flag covering the casket. Full military honours, the respectful gun salute before the final goodbye. A solitary bugler playing the Last Post. Alex's step-mother and award-winning film producer Veronica Blake Turner and his actor sisters Lucy Turner Briggs and

Georgina Turner Haigh cried rivers of tears between them. They never said anything to him, far too proud to reveal raw emotion, but each one of them must have secretly wished it was him the insurgents had hacked to pieces, not their son, their brother.

Turner knew better, ex-military made good in the security business, he understood combat, he understood life and he understood death.

He had told Jak after Alex's death that he would like to know what had really happened but there was no time limit, whenever Jak was ready to talk about it, he'd be there to listen.

First Jak had to escape the bottle that was sucking the life out him.

When he was sober and lucid before the service, Jak deflected the question about Alex and tried to explain to Turner that slaughtering children was the straw that broke the camel's back.

Whatever anyone's religion or belief system, how could you condone the murder of children? Turner was unequivocal.

It's the price of war Jak, the price of freedom Jak. Not your fault Jak. We've just paid the ultimate but it's always us or them. Don't take yourself too seriously. They fight dirty. Don't wear uniforms like we do. They mix in with the natives, Jak. Mix in so well you cannot be expected to differentiate. Swap sides as if they were playing a game of tag. Whoever offered them the best deal that day. They were that primitive Jak. Like the blacks in the oilfields of Africa, earning enough to feed themselves the next day before falling asleep wherever they stood. And them kids Jak, they're just as likely to detonate themselves as the other mad suicide fuckers. You walk away and you hold your head up high, you've done nothing wrong, no reason to be ashamed. You and Alex are heroes. Think of the lives you've saved. Think of the boys and girls in this great country of ours who sleep safe and sound because of what you've done. You won't understand now, you're grieving the loss of your best friend, my son, but when you do, I'll be here. You can rely on me Jak. You were the last person to see my son alive. You fought to save him. That's a unique bond no other two people on earth can ever share. You and me united forever by the death and our love of Alex, it is our destiny and our fate.

Not my fault.

Those were the words that stuck in his head before the binge started at Turner's country house where the bereaved father had hired a huge wedding marquee to say goodbye to his only son. His own personal jet helicopter parked alongside. Free drink for everyone and a diddly diddly band playing dance music until the early hours. Jak kept the irony of a previous enemy playing at the funeral of a soldier to himself.

Not my fault, he'd said when he'd finally sobered up in the clink and Turner was there agreeing, bailing him out and giving him a hand out until he was back on his feet again.

Turner nothing like his son had painted him. They would shake hands and Jak would be back down the pub drowning in drink while he adopted Turner's mantra of not taking himself too seriously.

Took a while to reach rock bottom and and take Turner's hand in friendship and not as an infinite source of blue drinking vouchers.

Not my fault.

Not your fault as Turner helped him rebuild his life and offered him a route to redemption.

All those random thoughts in the afterglow. He'd enjoyed her even if she did give him a hell of a whacking.

Should never have grabbed her hair.

She'd warned him fair and square but he'd wanted a bit of leverage for the last furlong prior to reaching the finishing post.

Ouch. Feisty bitch, he liked her.

He'd smiled after he'd come, until he realised he'd murdered a child.

Jak knew he'd have to cold turkey.

Avoid alcoholic annihilation and the ultimate meltdown, sucking deep on the cold metal barrel alone in a hotel room.

The sooner he was away from the city, the sooner he could cope with what he'd done.

Don't take yourself too seriously.

Not your fault.

Repeat ad infinitum.

Not my fault.
Not my fault
Not my fault.
Not my fault.

Possibly, probably.

He was undecided.

5: CHINA

Perched on the settee, China picks grit from Jak's damaged flesh to the sounds of Pink Floyd's musical essay on alienation, Wish Your Were Here.

China and Jak had compromised on the music if the volume was low.

Her tweezers dig out tiny stone fragments. Jak's butt naked, eyes fixed on the telly: *four dead in the city still, one a four year old boy.*

Does it hurt, she asked.

Only if you let it, he replied.

Do you want to talk about it, I'll listen without passing judgement, honest, she offered.

Judgement about what, he asked.

She nods towards the giant plasma. *Four dead?*

It's always easier to share a problem. Her right hand roams over his flat abdomen. Dabs iodine on his wounds with the other. He refuses to wince or continue with that conversation thread. Sorry about your hair, you nearly broke my ribs, he said, without the faintest hint of sarcasm. Is she clutching at straws or is this real? He'd burst Switchblade's bubble. Eddie quick to flick and red mist at the slightest provocation, real or perceived. Eddie fucking off and ignoring Chip's order to stay at Candy's World. Eddie more scared of Jak than Chip.

It's a wig, she said, my mask to protect me from this nightmare I inhabit. Pull it off and underneath I am all mush.

His hand glides over long legs trained for the Great Escape. Get it wrong and Danny's got company, wherever they disposed of him. Brave impetuous, impulsive Danny, challenging Chip for her freedom and losing.

How do you know Chip, she asked.

I don't, what's he to you, asked Jak.

He'll tell you he's my benefactor, my employer, my guardian, my mentor, amongst other things, said China, unable to state the bleeding obvious. It is too stark. Too upsetting. Me and Rose stay here rent free. Nice pad but I could do with a change. And chucking in my job.

Doing, asked Jak.

Doing.... A good question Jak, applying tweezers to his grazed thigh. I hawk sex, she said.

A hooker, he asked.

No, a bit more upmarket but not much. On a scale of one to ten, I operate at a pretty base level. I am a producer, a one time actress. This is a studio, specialising in wank movies when it's not my home. Least that was its intention before property diverted my business partners away from the adult film industry, said China.

You don't seem embarrassed, said Jak.

Why should I? Better than the minimum wage. Same rates as pole dancing, better hours. Not as good as a lawyer, an accountant or an assassin? Killing earns more than fucking or producing or directing people fucking each other.

She inspects her handiwork. She would have made a good nurse in another life. The wounds look clean.

Open up to me, she thinks, you must want to talk about it, knowing she is talking excessively herself.

Unable to find the pause button for her motormouth. Excited by the possibilities, knowing she is in danger of excessive recklessness.

Her big question; *when to pitch, when to ascertain if he was the Real Deal, a Guardian Angel sent from a Superior Force that she refused point blank to believe existed, the Interventionist God a group of girls had once discussed in the early hours after a Big Night Out.*

I loved having you inside me, she said. Makes me feel rampant. You're huge. Did you…she asked, fishing for compliments.

Normally it's men wanting a score out of 10. Was I the best, was I the biggest, the hardest, how many times did you come?

A finger gently touches her lips. Stops her from continuing. It is what it is, he said. No more. No less. A bodily function.

Want to go again, she asked.

Later, he said, you mentioned food.

Whatever you want. Quick food or an hour for the chilli or bolognese like I just said. Beer. Cider. Wine. A bit of blow to take the edge off. Whatever you want, said China. I am at your disposal.

I don't drink or smoke. Not anymore. Could do with making a call, he said, looking down at her, unconcerned about his nakedness, his ice cold blue eyes fixing on hers. Chip demanded radio silence, said China.

How will he know, he asked.

Chip knows everything, she replied.

Fuck him. By the time Mister Chippy looks at the bill, I'll be long gone, he said.

You don't know him like I do, said China.

A choice. Play the game Chip's way. Do as he instructed. VIP guest treatment. Or make her play and gamble her life and Rose's on the toss of a coin, the twist of a card, the spin of a roulette wheel.

She turns up Floyd as they have a cigar.

She's got smoking of her own to do.

Kiss me, she said, not sure if it was a demand or a question. Still uncertain, still unsure about her commitment. She removes a skin tight black lycra top, slender thin fingers snake his barrel chest.

She kisses him full on the lips.

She never kisses normally.

They are never given lightly.

Pulls his body into hers.

Careful not to make contact with his wounds.

Nestles her head into his shoulder.

Nips at him with her teeth.

Tiny bites.

Shoulder, neck, ear lobe.

Mirrors have eyes and ears, she whispered, holding his head in her hands.

His hands on her head, drawing her back.

Cameras behind the mirrors, Chip has ears and eyes everywhere. The music muffles our talking. Our pleasure. He watches all the time. He's evil. Really evil. The longer you stay, the longer you're a sitting duck. Me too. He'll kill us both, she said. What are we going to do?

6: JAK

The girl is smoking him, slowly, expertly, teasing him intensely, tiny spasms ripple through his body.

She is as good at her job as he is at his, or was, before he topped a four year old child.

She's whispering to him but he's not really listening.

Not his fault. Not his fault.

He needs to be away now.

What had she called this place? Candy's World.

Sounded like an adventure park for children, not a skin flick factory to satisfy blokes tossing themselves off in dark rooms knee deep in kleenex. Not that it mattered. He wanted out now, not waiting for dusk to fall.

How stupid was that? In a war zone yes. In a city with a million plus people? Madness.

When she was finished, he'd call Turner to fast forward

the exit and then the cold turkey could begin without her relentless conversation.

Turner had been true to his word about his offer of redemption and a fresh start.

He helped Jak enrol on an AA 12 step programme, found him an apartment in the village nearest to his estate.

Turner took Jak on a few business trips and networked with movers and shakers who offered lucrative opportunities to former snipers.

There were a couple of short stints bodyguarding in the Middle East where the pay was good, the hours arduous and the work dangerous.

He was surrounded by semi-professional incompetents, adrenaline death wish junkies and shattered undiagnosed alcoholics diving into and dying in a bottle, like Eddie after the mass killings, his fear understandable, except he was a jerk off artist and a yellow bully.

When Jak found himself in a Dubai hotel with a gun and a bottle, he called Turner, his bodyguarding career over. Turner shrugged off the disappointment, who wants to be the richest man in the cemetery, he'd said.

Not your fault.

Turner and Jak hung out while he got re-established on God's 12 steps, staring the bottle down like they would the enemy before they crossed a battle's start line.

As always, Turner reminded Jak he would like to know the real truth about Alex but Jak knew if he did he would not like it.

They visited the set of a swashbuckling pirate movie as guests of Turner's glam award winning film producer wife Veronica Turner Blake, all of them flying in low by helicopter from the family estate, swapping chit chat with movie stars and celebs, bypassing the booze and drugs on constant offer, like croissants and coffee for breakfast in a posh hotel.

Filming was as boring as lying in an observation post for three days in a wet diddly diddly paddy potato field.

Veronica, who looked like a film star herself, offered Jak stunt work when one of the film guys broke his leg falling from the rigging of a replica wooden ship. Well paid work but it involved water scenes and he'd never liked getting wet, not that he would let on.

Finally Turner hit upon the solution: go back to doing what you do best. What's that, Jak had asked. Shooting people, said Turner. We'll have to stop being seen together in public but I'll commission you on behalf of our 'syndicate'. You'll get associate membership, your guaranteed 'get-out-of-jail-free' card.

He'd gone along with Turner's suggestion, asked what it would cost him. Turner said 40% of his earnings and his conscience. Turner said he could build up a pile of cash and start a new life one day. How will I know when the time is right to start a new life, Jak asked. When you're ready to tell me exactly how Alex really died, not the sanitised PR version for the authorities but the truth, the real truth, only the truth, then you're ready to discard the past and move on.

Jak had said yes, not touched a drop since and never seen Turner face to face although they often spoke by phone, which sort of made keeping Alex's confession secret a lot easier.

Since then, he'd killed six people without any problem. No comeback legally or morally. Surprised he'd grown into the role so smoothly, his only disaster this job.

It had been extremely short notice but Turner had vouched for the client, a very good friend with impeccable credentials.

One of us, someone who could be trusted.

One person Jak should never have trusted was the middle

aged bloke dressed in his own branded golfing merchandise, Chip Mackie. Didn't like his two hooded associates either, one now dead, the other festering in his own excrement. Daft jerks with their hoodies and Madchester t-shirts and low slung jeans even though both were knocking late thirties, early forties.

Jak should have known they could not organise the proverbial piss-up in a brewery.

He should have insisted on a sniper shoot.

Chip had said no, it had to be now. They had a location and a time. He'd do the deed and they'd keep him safe until it was dark when he could slip away unnoticed. Jimmy and Eddie had both said to Chip that they didn't need an outsider doing the job, that they could do it themselves. Ride up and pop, pop, pop, job's a good 'un. At the time he'd laughed and asked the two brothers if they'd ever killed before. Us to know you to find out, Eddie had replied, puffing up his chest so it matched the size of his ample gut.

Jak had apologised for wasting everyone's time, said it was clear they didn't need him and if they could drop him back at the airport and cover his expenses then it could be put down to 'experience'.

Why didn't he walk? He owed Turner and felt obligated to stay and listen.

Jimmy will ride up on the bike and I'll pop the bald jerk, Eddie had said, it's a plan that Ged would back Chip, you know it. Call him.

Chip tried and failed, the embarrassed silence punctuated by the grinning buffoon brothers hopping from one undone trainer to the other undone trainer. I'll treble your money, said Chip, direct to you, no middlemen, pay up this afternoon before you leave. But you do it like Jimmy and Eddie recommend. Eddie spots. Jimmy rides. You shoot.

With hindsight it was obvious it was going to backfire,

bound to go wrong. A four year old child and his mother and father leave their house for an afternoon in the city centre, a walk in the park. A bite to eat, family fun. Never expecting for one second to be gunned down in the street, never expecting life to end so abruptly.

Not his fault.

If you said it often enough and with enough conviction you could blame everyone else.

Not his fault. Like it wasn't his fault lying side by side with Alex, hidden on the side of a mountain, using telescopic sights to track a little boy happily herding goats.

He should have refused but treble money for an afternoon's work was good business that would keep Turner happy.

So he'd asked them about the weapon.

They'd gone to the back of Chip's black off-road vehicle with tinted black windows and a CHIP1 personalised number plate. We've hired it by the day, said Chip, hence the urgency.

Does it work, Jak had asked as he inspected the clean, well-oiled unit. He dismantled the gun, field stripping and reassembling it with professional ease.

The gun was good. Like she was good. Very good. Whatever her name was. He hadn't asked. She hadn't offered. If Eddie had used it, the name had by-passed him.

Ammunition, Jak had asked. Chip held out his hand, grinning.

Five hollow Black Talon bullets with black Lubalox coating. Jak had seen them used by wannabes full of shit gleaned from the internet, expanding rounds that messed people up. A scary bullet by reputation rather than design.

There was better ammo on the market but Black Talons sounded evil and looked nastier, clever branding creating an intimidating illusion.

Only five, he'd asked Chip.

How many shots do you need? Thought you were professional, replied Chip.

We're good to go I suppose, Jak said, seeing the look of satisfaction on Chip's face.

He was a very worried man despite his veneer of outer calmness. He looked like shit too, combusting internally, heart and blood pressure bubbling under.

Good to go, that's what I like to hear. Let's do it, said Chip, fatal last words for a four year old boy.

Not his fault. Not his fault at all.

He stroked her false hair.

Was she was on the house or would she give him a bill for personal services.

He didn't mind, she'd been worth it.

Let her polish him off then he'd call Turner to rescue him before he accepted her offer of a first drink on the road to ruin and damnation.

7: CHIP

Chip checks the live stream on his mobile. They are at it again, like bloody rabbits. It disgusts him. Is she acting or is it for real? And him? Turner's monkey was an animal. Wrecking ball was a good description of his talents with a gun and a conch. Chip is in the Paradise Hills resort's 19th hole, sat in a corner of the golf bar, above him a huge framed oil painting he'd commissioned of himself lifting a crystal glass trophy against the stunning backdrop of a Shanghai setting sun, his first tour victory achieved in his early twenties. Sally Bailey, the PR, Anna Judd, the journalist and John second name unknown, the photographer, are busy powdering their noses, hair of the dog. On the small mobile screen Turner's monkey is flopped out on the large black settee, China's head bobbing up and down between his legs with an energy and enthusiasm missing from her movies. He'd let her adopt slack work practices, daft soft beggar that he was, on account of the distractions of the resort.

No apologies, the easy money of the Paradise Hills' project encouraged him to take his eye off the ball. Easy money, that was a joke. Sex always paid more consistently, just not as big as the massive profits offered up by commercial property investments. Spooky techhead Denzil Grant had rigged cameras behind the mirrors at Candy's World to stream real time encrypted data. He didn't know how Denzil fixed things, only appreciated he did. As long as Ged assured Chip it was safe and secure, he was happy. He'd trust Ged with his life. They had numerous unedited hours of 'voyeur' footage ready to be exploited, although he was not sure how much people would pay to see China run on a treadmill, cook or chase Rose before bathtime. There was always a market for the latter. China and Rose, mother and daughter. Both wilful. Like China's mother, an American college girl with a swing as dazzling as her smile. She the product of rich parents and a golfing scholarship to a top university. He the polar opposite; humble beginnings, semi-skilled working class roots he'd long since disowned, an education that started behind the bicycle shed and ended on the golf course when he discovered he could control the movement of a small white ball over huge and short distances. China, like her mother, was a silly girl. Shame of it all was no matter how much you gave and they took, it was never enough. If he turned up the volume, she'd be playing her music while she worked the monkey spanker. Her playlists capture her moods apparently. Music from before she was even born. Wearing her wig as if that disguised the fact she wasn't a very silly girl, a major disappointment. A protege who blew a very serious talent in a sea of wilfulness, a paranoid liar with a vicious forked tongue who could not be trusted. He called her the Girl Who Cried Wolf to the Merry Men. They laughed and nodded, lap dogs who knew what side their bread was buttered. Only Danny had disagreed, getting all macho and confronting him with his hackles raised. Silly young fool. Never asked Ged what he had done with the body and the information had never been volunteered. Ged was good like that. Chip had had a serious word with China in the bathroom, almost miscalculated his warning shot as the blood drained out of her small breasts, large feet and long fingers. Was she going to try it on with Turner's monkey? Why could she never learn the lessons about family etiquette? Why had she transformed herself from a beautiful pretty young butterfly to a bitter, cynical bitch intent on causing him nothing but trouble. It gave him a headache thinking about her.

He stopped the video steam and called up Amy from half an hour earlier. Such a great little swing, compact and complete. She was the future. Rose was the future. China the past. China bored him. Wore him out. Maybe it was time to kiss her goodbye. Ask Eddie to sort it out, wherever he was. He flips back from Amy's swing to Candy's World. Where was Eddie? The monkey and China are still rabbiting away. Where was Eddie, jacking off, bashing his bishop? Is he watching the two rabbits? Surprised he's not made it a threesome, beast that he is. He calls up the dashboard. Looks in all the rooms, upstairs and downstairs. Eddie is not there.

The glassy-eyed media duo are back, sitting themselves down at the table in the 19th hole, grinning away inanely, cocained off their tits. Why do they call you Chip, Chip, asked a giggling Anna, hacking him off more than she could ever imagine. He offers her a crisp and resists the temptation when she places it in her delicate upper class mouth. Where is Eddie? Where's bloody Eddie? His migraine returns. This is all China's fault. Her and that idiot she's banging. His patience was being severely tested.

8: DEEKS

An open palm slams the black door inwards. Is the washroom empty?

No time to ascertain. Sink or toilet? A split second to decide, equidistance. Practicalities say the latter, easier to tidy up afterwards. A slim manila A4 folder is sent flying into the corner of the room. A black Doc Martin shoe kicks open the cubicle door, grazed knees hit cold black tiles, the pain goes unnoticed. Grazed hands lift the black plastic toilet seat, grasp cold white porcelain. Stomach heaves violently, hurling up half digested food.

First time sick on the job, two decades in.

Chucks on empty, praying nobody comes in and sees a senior police officer exposed and vulnerable. Bum high in the air, head thrust down a toilet.

It's OK, no one else is watching officer collapse this afternoon. The throw-up cop will not be televised or appear on You Tube for the world's viral amusement.

Deeks flushes sick from the toilet, cleans around the rim. Mops up the bits missed, flushes again. Stands on unsteady pins and walks to the sink, stares at a shattered translucent ghost in the mirror, black dishevelled hair matted with Cindy's blood and brains.

A quick finger nail inspection.

Cut short but room enough to collect bits of Cindy. No brushes to scrub them in the toilet. Deeks believed tidy manicured hands said a lot about a person. Like regularly brushed teeth. Fresh breath. Ironed clothes. An absence of body odour. Nicotine breath and the lingering stench of stale alcohol. Too many officers never cared about the basics. Deeks' fingers were always immaculate so it couldn't be anything else other than Cindy's gunk that had emptied out of her shattered skull.

Heaves on empty again in response to the visual image.

Grips the sink to stay upright. Looks at the folder on the floor. Why is there no training on God's earth to tell you how to cope when you've failed to stop blood and brain erupting like lava from a gaping hole in a shattered skull? How are you meant to react to a colleague's vacant eyes unable to comprehend what has just happened?

Words?

What words of comfort could possibly be offered when the candle dims and is about to stop burning?

Hang on in there? What bloody nonsense was that all about? Hang on in where? Help is at hand? Poppycock.

The assassin had been ten feet away, maximum twelve, thirteen.

Unlucky for Cindy. Plump, sexy, sassy Cindy. Cindy no more. Popular effervescent Cindy, with more friends than most, boys and girls who loved her vitality and wit. The assassin with his gun already raised. Cindy, stupid daft, impulsive; Cindy had reacted first, pushed herself between the target and the gunman. Why not just stand there Cindy and let it happen? What was the point of a posthumous medal for swallowing bullets intended for a paedo? Your family cannot put their arms around a gong. Your friends cannot dance around memories in a nightclub, pissing themselves with laughter, wrapping themselves around lap dancing poles to imitate the one girl who could do it properly.

Deeks had seen it unfold from forty yards, oblivious to the dangers. Coming down the steps of the building, hacked off at the rank pulling by Serious Crimes. Harry Wade all apologetic, shrugging broad shoulders, really sorry but ultimately Chris DeVeres is too important for Serious Crimes to pass. He's ours.

Wrong there buddy. He was their sting. Their catch. Their deviant. Their paedo.

Nothing to do with Harry Wade or Serious Crimes or anybody else.

Paedos were like double decker buses. Wait an age to catch one and another half a dozen expose themselves in the mop up operation. Paedos. They rarely operated alone, preferring to feed off each other like pirañas. Until Harry Wade and Serious Crimes commandeered their catch, of course. Ruined the sting operation. Insisted he was moved across the city into their protection. Deeks had argued but not hard enough. Cindy was gone, destined for the mortuary slab. Deeks had ceded ground far too easily. Far too meekly. Far too fatally. Harry Wade had trampled steel-toe-capped shoes all over the Sex Crimes team. Invaded their territory. Uninvited. Their paedo trap. A 54 year old man pretending to be a 15 year old skateboarder. Chatting up a 28 year old female police constable imitating a vulnerable 13 year old teenager desperately seeking attention. Both were gone, Cindy and paedo.

How many shots were discharged?

Hard to remember.

Not allowed to investigate.

Not allowed to chase the cowardly cunt. The bastard cold as you like. Pulled up his visor. Raised the gun and fired through Cindy, soon-to-be-married and honeymooning in Antigua Cindy. Wife-to-be for Richard, the insurance salesman who would now be considerably richer once, or if, he got over the grief. Cindy mother-to-be-for-no-one-no-more. The assassin had fired through her head in cold blood, knew exactly what he was doing. For Deeks running to the incident was the only response. Fuck taking cover. Fuck self-preservation. An officer fucking down. Deeks moving towards Cindy and simultaneously watching the motorbike reversing back into the road. Thinking. Assessing. Calculating. The paedo gone. Christian DeVeres. 54. A Chartered Management Accountant. Number cruncher by trade. Lots of letters after his name. A wife and three children. All boys. Golf club member. Charity fund raiser. Child groomer stung. Thinking Cindy, poor soon-to-be-buried-or-cremated Cindy, was a 13 year old schoolgirl 'turned on' talking online to Ryan Dowling aka 'BudgieBoy' aka Chris with half his head missing. Thinking human bodies have an awful lot of blood inside them and most of Cindy's was flooding the pavement. Of course, it was poetic justice in a stupid, dumb way, except he would never be held to account or have his day of shame in the courts. His whole fucking life a total fake, a pillar of the community who would avoid a paedo child molesting motherfucker epitaph unless they spread the rumours themselves when they chucked him six feet down in the clay. Deeks hated, and hated was the operative word, hated men who abused children. Nothing worse. A blight on humanity. All of us for letting it happen. Me, you, him and her. Deeks turned down promotions to chase fucking paedos. Everyone else said it was just a job. There was more to a full and happy life than relentlessly chasing child abusers. Money to be earned. Power to be deployed. Holidays in the sun. Smart cars. Designer watches and suits. Look at Harry Wade. Man on the move. Saw Harry every day. He was indeed a man on the move. Addicted to the promotion bug. Talked about little else. Look at Harry Wade they would say. Fuck Harry. Look at Cindy hanging on, thrashing, reminiscent of a deep sea fishing trip, a team building exercise. The first mackerel plucked from the sea, left to suffocate in a scruffy red plastic washing up bowl. An ignominious and lonely death as it flapped and flapped. Then their mutual immunity to the suffering as other mackerel were added, sheer numbers sanitising the death thrash. One death a tragedy, many a statistic. Cindy, daughter, sister, niece and aunt, friend and colleague; body broken, spirit leaving the beautiful human podgy shape that was once Cindy. A couple of months ago, an engagement party with her friends, a pole dancing club, one of them swinging around like it was an Olympic sport. Deeks had expected to see them all again at the wedding, not her funeral.

Some Cindy talking.

Not anymore. Reacting to Cindy's plight. Attempting to push warm brain back into the cavity from where it came, just in case. Just in case? Just in case God wanted to change the habit of a lifetime and perform an interventionist miracle. In the wee wee hours talking to Cindy and her drunken friends about an interventionist God. Torch singer Nick Cave and his chilled out Black Seeds sang Into My Arms over the PA. Staff slowly closed the nightclub and offered the exhausted girls pots of strong black coffee. An interventionist God? A split giggling decision. No lessons in standing orders about how to deal with the death of a colleague and a friend, murdered on a late wet Sunday morning on the wet streets of a wet cold dour northern city. Sirens wailing, help coming but not soon enough. No way. Hang in there Cindy, although she's already going, going, gone, the auctioneer's gavel taps out the final three beats. The candle blown out in the wind on a cold wet Sunday in a cold, wet city, like the one you live in. Deeks knowing. Multi-tasking. Comforting. Witnessing. Deeks watching the motorbike wheel away at high speed. Rubber skidding on wet slippy tarmac. Helpless to stop the assassin's escape from the carnage he has created. Remembering again, a casual assassin moments after the kill. He glanced over as Deeks reached Cindy. Never to be forgotten ice cold light blue eyes admiring his handy work.

Stop them, Deeks screamed, a voice lost in the chaos. I'll remember you. I'll never forget your fucking eyes. As the bike races away, somebody up there must have heard the shout. Must have felt bad about letting Cindy go in such an awful way. God? Jesus? The Holy Ghost? An interventionist superior being was a good thing to believe in, Deeks always thought.

The motorbike slides on wet tarmac. The motorcyclist loses control, slaloms into the path of an oncoming green double decker bus. The bike misses. The head of the cyclist doesn't ... the helmet rolling like a football...is the head still inside it? Thank you. Justice for Cindy. Immediate divine retribution. You're a witness. Notice these things. The passenger helped to his feet and dragged away. Deeks felt only disappointment a car didn't crush his body on a wet street of a wet city on a wet Sunday morning; a time when people should be reading the papers and drinking coffee and chatting about their busy, uncomplicated lives, you and me included.

Deeks bends down and picks up the folder thrown into the corner of the toilet. You're a witness. Stay at the station until you're interviewed. But we need to help. Deeks, do what you're told. A red tape jobsworth playing it by the rule book.

Deeks pushes the pictures back into the folder. Independent complaints sticking their oar in where it was not wanted, slowing everything down to a virtual standstill. Colour returns to the face that stares back from the toilet mirror hanging on a black and white tiled wall. If only life was that simple. Everything black and white. Yes or no? Innocent or guilty?

Five minutes earlier.

The team minus Cindy. Alan 'Minty' Green, Clive Dobson, Phil Ash and Ed Boucher. Each one tried and trusted, each one incapable of betraying the cause? The head said yes. The gut? The gut was undecided. All of them sat in the office. Four when it should have been five. Cindy the youngest, the least experienced. Cindy, laughing, joking, always game Cindy, a popular team player. Spurred on to catch paedos like Deeks because she believed it made the world a better place. Deeks would often quote the long dead persecuted comedian Lenny Bruce. *One person, nine people. Anything goes with sex as long as it is not with children. Never, ever with children. There was never any exception.* Why would anyone want to involve children? A child? What possible reason? None of them would try to answer, ever. Deeks. Minty. Ash, Dobbo and Bouch. Only knew they wanted to catch the bastards. All of them in a state of shock. Sat there, unable to articulate anything beyond coffee and tea requests and swapping tabs. The room hazy with tobacco smoke. Like the old days. Before everyone went PC. They, whoever they were, said passive smoking would kill you. Wrong. Bloody bullets killed you, but only if someone pointed a gun, knows the target, knows who to kill and when. Fuck health and safety. Fuck everyone. Fuck everything. Itching to join the chase. Confined to a smoky windowless office because they were all fucking witnesses. Choking in their frustration.

Then the massive realisation. Only if someone points the gun. The sickness an automatic reaction. Leaving the room calm and assured. Coping with death was part of the group leader's job description. Knowing who caused it was another matter. Another gut reaction. Understanding the implications. Oblivious to the obvious in the immediate aftermath of the bloodbath. The opportunity so tight. The window so small. The odds of a random attack? Zero. Only one realistic explanation.

Senses working overtime.

Baited.

Child groomer Chris DeVeres messaging Cindy. His webcam was bust. But his mum and dad would get it fixed. Rely on them. They were cool. Yes, he'd show her his just as soon as they did. Asking her to inspect her *gash*, his word not Cindy's. A red light word. *Gash* not youth street talk in the city. *Gash* belonged to another time, another place, an older generation. BudgieBoy aka Reg prompted and probed 28 year old Cindy to describe her special place. Asked her to play with her wet *gash* so they could share the pleasure. Told her he loved her. She meant the world to him. They would be together for eternity. Show me your secret place between your soul and your spirit. Show me your cunt on camera and in the real world. Too shy today? I'll book a hotel room and I'll meet you there and we'll explore our bodies in the flesh.

Hooked.

Chris following the directions to the tee. Chris expecting to meet a child and being greeted by Deeks and the rest of the team in the hotel room. Chris at first chuckling, a high falsetto laugh directed at the adults in front of him. A great joke. Not very funny. Not funny at all. It's not April Fool's Day, it's not my birthday, I've not been promoted because I am my own boss. Great idea of a wind up but I am a busy man. I am here to meet the Kh.... stopping mid-sentence as the realisation dawns on his fat, bald face that he's in trouble. His weedy eyes computing behind spectacles with thick lenses. Minty reading him his rights as they arrest him, Deeks slipping on the cuffs, always carries two pairs, always revelling in cuffing the bastards. That's when the paedos knew they were in deep shit. Course, it would change once the lawyers and the CPS got involved and convictions depended on who could hire the most expensive barristers to con the jury.

Wriggling.

Deeks watching the team firing questions at him. Like a job interview, simple questions initially to confirm his identity.

Name.

Age.

Date of birth.

Address.

Occupation.

Place of work.

Chris DeVeres answered without fear, unlike other paedophiles ensnared in honeytraps, not in the least bit intimidated. Then the questions got a bit more personal, a little trickier. The humour and the high falsetto replaced by a deadpan no comment, eyes down.

Did he have a computer?

No comment.

Did he have access to the internet?

No comment.

Did he meet people for sex on the internet?

No comment.

Did he use internet chatrooms to meet people on the internet?

No comment.

Did he use the username BudgieBoy?

No comment.

Did he ever chat to a schoolgirl aged 13 with the username AprilShowers?

No comment.

Did he arrange to meet her for sex?

No comment.

If not, why was he at the hotel?

No comment.

Who did he expect to meet at the hotel?

No comment.

Had he come to have sexual intercourse with a girl he knew to be thirteen years old?

No comment.

Had he groomed her and other underage girls for sex?

No comment.

They give him a break from Minty and Ash; Bouch and Dobbo's turn for their *we're your friends not fiends* chit chat over coffee and croissants. They tell him he levels with them, they'll look after him. All he has to do is confess and supply the names of others who endanger vulnerable children. Nothing could be easier. He'd be home for tea, nobody any the wiser. Might even escape a custodial, a slap on the wrist, a few hours community service and a spell on the sex register. They'd do their damnedest to keep it out of the media too.

Another switch and lewd transcripts of intimate internet conversations with a 13 year old schoolgirl are read out to him by Minty and Ash. Graphic sexual requests accompanied by links and references to songs and poems about eternal deep rooted love. Are you denying you've not tried to groom underage girls for sexual gratification they ask Chris, as he looks blankly at the floor and reiterates his no comment rap, before adding that he'd like to make a call, which he believed was his legal right.

Several hours pass before they finally relent by which time they've obtained a search warrant, raided his home and his office and taken his computers and other items of interest to help with their investigations. You can make your call now they tell him, hardly able to hide their disappointment that he never coughed. Chris calls a Peer of the Realm, Hugh 'Bing' Bingham, one of his clients, a close personal family friend and an intimate of the country's Number One Family. Within half a day of making that call DeVeres is shot dead on a wet street in a wet city on a wet Sunday late morning.

Off the hook.

45 minutes after the call request, Harry and two detectives from serious crimes turn up for private conversations with Chris. Another 45 minutes and Harry changes the rules: he's ours. We're taking him into witness protection. On what evidence? Don't compromise our ongoing investigations, don't get ideas above your rank. All the time Deeks thinking no way to speak to me. Talk to you later about this. I won't forget. No Sir. I won't forget. On neutral territory buddy.

On homeground. We'll resolve this. Knowing it would never happen. Harry was fast tracking too fast, networked and school-tied to the eyeballs.

You lot. I am seeing Harry Wade. Going to discuss the case while it's still raw and untainted by time. What's going on, they ask in unison, suspicious Deeks was consorting with the 'enemy' so soon after the death of Cindy. Yes, I am consorting with the 'enemy' but I am not telling you lot why, thought Deeks. Remember your A-levels. Books the size of fucking house bricks. William fucking Thackeray and Vanity Fair - Dickens and Bleak House - and bloody WH Auden - a white feather runaway coward who fucked off 3,000 miles to avoid the Nazis - didn't read his drivel on principle. But Hamlet. Hamlet was different. That was good. That was cool. The play within a play to trap a king who killed a king. The plan was simple: entice Harry Wade to trap Harry Wade. A good plan. Deeks gave them their instructions.

Our contact is still 'live'. The case does not, will not, die with him. Not today. Not tonight. Not tomorrow. Every detail about the life and times of Christian DeVeres needs to be investigated. Every call and every email traced and matched to a human with a face and a home address. I want to know Chris inside out so it feels like I am wearing his slimy paedo skin over my own. No detail too small. Every person suspect. Why? Why. Why? Because Cindy is shot dead on our watch, said Deeks, rummaging in a filing cabinet, looking for images that would shatter your heart into a thousand broken pieces. Like it had done to Cindy's so many times before the candle blew out on a wet Sunday in a city just like mine and yours.

9: CHINA

Silence in the afterglow. Pink Floyd no longer Wish You Were Here. The album climaxed as he did. While the last bars play themselves out, China is held in Jak's muscular arms. He's half asleep, breathing lightly, verging on a slight snore. A reassuring warmth emanates from his torso. She responds, snuggly fitting into his shape, clutching to him tightly with long limbs, a koala clinging to a eucalyptus tree. She likes koala bears with their good parenting skills, carrying, feeding and protecting their young. Rose thought they were cute too. Had a couple of stuffed koalas in her bedroom. She had lots of toys. In reality, koalas were vicious creatures with sharp lethal claws. Shred you to threads in seconds should you threaten them or their young. She wishes she had that ability. China feels herself start to drift away and pinches her wrist hard to snap herself awake. There is a small, very small, window of opportunity. She has to befriend a mass murderer. Yes, he's shot dead four people but he is her self-appointed White Stallion Man. Although he has no idea about her plans, she's already made the decision: *he is the chosen one, the special one.* Way she sees it, he has already downloaded on her twice so he owes her Big Time. He just needs to be told once she has evolved a realistic exit plan for her and Rose to permanently erase Chip from contaminating their lives. Her problem was to convince Jak it was his plan, his idea. Men were like that, they wanted to be in control. Just the way they were. Dumb really but then life was stupid at the best of times. As she constantly reminded herself during her lowest moments: *we're just meat and bones hitching a ride on a rock speeding through space, nothing special. You could jump off anytime you wanted.* Except China had to look after her daughter, who had never asked to be born. But for Rose, she'd probably have chosen another way out, like her own mother. She was sure of that. Only Rose gave her hope. Only Rose gave her a future. Only with Rose could she dream beyond her home, her prison, her life sentence in purgatory. *A beach. Blue seas. Bright sun. Serving food in a restaurant next to golden sandy beaches.* Was that too much to ask after what she had suffered? She deserved compensation. And if they weren't going to volunteer it, she'd take it. But how to approach her break for freedom? What do you do next? She plays with time in her head. How do you measure, calculate or make sense of 15 million light years or the next crucial 60 minutes?

Jak's head rests on her shoulder. China inspects his face closely. The lines around his eyes put him in his forties, possibly late thirties. There is a day or two's stubble although his skin positively shines with good health, the opposite of bloated, rotting, rancid Switchblade Eddie. Jak smells like a real man should, doesn't reek of stale BO, booze, tobacco and ejaculate. Jak cares about how he looks and presents himself. She just had to convince him to care the same way about her and Rose. But how? His clothes are in the washing machine, a 60 minute cycle with the tumble dryer. How long had the frolic taken? A 45 minute album played through from start to finish. On the floor are her black lycra top and bottoms and black knickers and his CK boxers. White sports socks cover her overlarge feet, her worst feature in her eyes. They kind of embarrassed her. Stupid really. It was the least of her worries. Big feet. She smiles at the silliness of it all, aware she is actually relaxed, her body feels like it is drifting effortlessly through space. She'd never, she wasn't sure … only by herself. Had one sneaked up and caught her unawares or were freedom fantasies inducing unprecedented highs? Pull yourself together girl. Stop daydreaming. The big picture. Get serious. She has to engage him. They had temporarily bonded using the only currency that had appeared to matter in her short sad life: *fucking, sucking, sterile sex*. A chemical reaction that turned ordinary average men and women into monsters. Unlike others who could not clear off quick enough, Jak had clung to her afterwards. Shared the moment, shone in the afterglow, not wiped himself on a metaphorical curtain and tucked away the discharged weapon. His koala to her eucalyptus. Or was it vice versa. Whatever, it was a sign from her Guardian Angel, if she had one, that he was the one: her Heroic Horse Rider Mounted on a Magnificent White Charger. Jak Had the Power. The Sheer Will. The Lack of Fear. Two fingers lightly trace the laughter lines around his eyes. They open instantly. Perhaps he'd not been asleep at all. Merely pretending. He smiles. Good teeth up close. Possibly capped.

That was fun. I have to make a call he said, although he doesn't relinquish his grip on her body.

Chip's listening, like I said, before you wanted to frolic.

Twice in an hour, she whispered into his ear, unsure if her voice would be picked up. Scared that it would. She had the scars on her wrists to prove the fear was real enough.

So what, he whispered back, his guard apparently dropped in his own afterglow. The sooner I make the call, the sooner I am out of your hair, so to speak. A hand strokes the wig once again and pulls away just as quickly.

Chip says no contact. The minute you call, he'll know. Chip's bugged the whole house. Where there is a mirror there is a camera, she said.

Why, he asked.

Why indeed. White lies or truth, she asked herself. Do you run? Keep fit? Looks like you do. I'll race you on the treadmills. There's quarter of an hour for your washing to finish. That chilli will be ready at the same time or you can have bolognese. I have two special recipes. We'll do 5km. Loser has to do a forfeit, she grinned.

Don't be daft, he said.

Man or mouse, she asked. You scared a mere skinny underfed and oversexed slip of a woman will beat you. She broke the embrace, reached for her clothes, the plan crystallising in her grey matter. Get your keks on, said China, I am not running next to you with that big thing slapping against your legs. She'd said it without thinking. Sex compartmentalised, voice on automatic pilot, like the grunting Russian tennis player she became when the inner director shouted Camera Lights Action.

Forfeit. I've already.... said Jak, faltering, possibly at the crassness of the remark.

Been fucked and sucked by me. Missed another hole out, she said. Saw him flinch at the starkness.

And if you win, he asked.

Easy, she said, you kill Chip and Ged Grant for me and anyone else who gets in our way.

10: DEEKS

Christ what happened to you, you look like death warmed up, said Harry Wade, inappropriate and insensitive as usual.

You were there, you saw the whole bloody slaughter, although you left early, said Deeks.

I had no choice, said Harry. I was the senior officer and had to assume command back at HQ until I could hand over. You understand don't you?

Sure, said Deeks, watching Harry Wade rise from behind his big executive desk, the size of a football goalmouth. What was wrong with a normal desk?

Sorry about your loss, said Harry.

Our, it's our, loss, Cindy was our loss, one of us, not mine, said Deeks.

She'll be missed, she was a good officer, said Harry.

Cindy good? Bollocks, thought Deeks. Cindy was a crap officer. A dead policewoman with a bullet smashed through

64

her skull and her brains under my nails was not a good officer. What use was she dead? How could she entrap paedos six feet under? Couldn't do anything now except attract false pity from Harry and other senior officers feigning compassion when the cameras were on and indifference when they weren't. Deeks knew they thought self-awareness was for bleeding hearts.

Yes Sir, she'll be missed, said Deeks.

You could have changed. You look like shit, said Harry.

I tried to save her Sir. Tried to stop her brains decorating the city's streets Sir, said Deeks.

Call me Harry. Everyone else does, said Harry, their private joke.

We're on duty. Feels awkward Sir. Difficult since we both, said Deeks, leaving the rest unspoken.

You should have changed. I insist, said Harry. Go home and change. No one is going to think any the less of you. No badges for wearing the debris of a colleague all over yourself. But don't start changing in here. Give people the wrong idea. You know how they talk.

Deeks breaks into a rueful smile while brash Harry smooth talks on automatic pilot. Carefully, Deeks places the manila folder on his outsized executive desk. DO NOT REMOVE: STRICTLY CONFIDENTIAL. Deeks knows the large black type will intrigue Harry Wade, same as placing a big, juicy meaty bone in front of a ravenous dog. Have you got a spare top in your sports bag, she asked, instigating the play within a play to trap a Wade. Harry loved to play sport. Squash. Badminton. The gym. Exercise made you a better officer was his mantra. Exercise the body and you exercise the mind. Deeks knew Harry considered himself a philosopher. He would tell her confidentially that he was planning a self-help book on the social responsibilities of the police beyond catching criminals. Deeks slowly undid the buttons on the blood and brain splattered white blouse. Watching Harry watching her as if she was about to take the dogs for a stroll across the park. Lifting her tight black Versace skirt up around her hips to pull down blood and brain splattered torn black tights. Watching Harry watching her as if she was about to defecate, innocently scratching an imaginary itch on her black lace panties with a tiny bow above the crotch. Watching Harry watching her as if she was about to remove a full tampon. The top Harry? Any would do. He always had plenty of spares. Harry sweated like a pig when he exerted himself or when he was outside of his comfort zone. Possibly the one black feather in his cap that could derail his ascent. Sweating didn't look good on telly, made you look sly and untrustworthy. You got a top, she repeated. Any would do. They were roughly the same size. Both touching on or just over six foot. She didn't do the squash or the badminton. Swimming, running and cycling were her releases from work pressures. Swimming first and foremost. Broad shoulders and hardly any boobs were the price of being a water babe, a GB waterpolo player in her teens before career and parenting changed her focus. Deeks slipped out of the silk blouse, the white bra effortlessly holding in two small handfuls. Not strictly needed. It never bothered Deeks. Others demanded manmade silicon chests, paid through the nose for them. She was happy with what God gave her. She could never understand the fascination. Men were gullible when it came to sex, most of them leastways. Harry hadn't been for a long time. There wasn't one iota of lust in his eyes as she slowly stripped, inspected the white bra for splashes of blood and brain after she'd taken it off. Harry hurriedly throws her a green and yellow hoodie from his red sports bag. She catches it and in return throws him the white bra. Tells him to put it straight in the bin alongside the white blouse and the ruined black tights.

Could never wear them again, not with Cindy's remains caked all over them. Deeks cups her tiny poached eggs, squeezes them together gently, what some might consider to be an arousing gesture. Watching Harry look beyond her as if she was eating her own excrement. Still topless, she points to the file on the desk, knowing he is itching to have a butchers. Take a look inside, she said. Might help us understand Chris DeVeres. Deeks hooks the green and yellow hoodie over her head and looks at her own reflection in a large plate glass window. Yes, she was still sexually attractive. If Harry didn't like her body, others did. Men wanted sex with her. She was proud of how she looked and how she kept in shape and remained sexually active and adventurous. It wasn't easy balancing a high powered job with motherhood. Career opportunities and breeding were not conducive to maintaining a svelte-like figure. Awful isn't it, she said to Harry, explaining he was looking at Grade 9 images of children with penetrative adults. Watching Harry inspecting the images, slowly checking image after image after image, forgetting himself. Deeks had seen many others unacquainted with child abuse view similar images, knows their instinctive response is utter revulsion. Most can only view one or two before stopping and saying it is too much, too awful, too soul destroying. Not Harry. No Sir. The immediate repulsion was missing. The instinctive knee-jerk rejection to the sheer horror of the images wasn't in him. Deeks watching him watching them. Deeks knew. Deeks bloody well knew. Take me home Harry, I am exhausted, she said. Harry looked up, a sheen of sweat glistening on his entire face. His eyes glazed like he'd been drugged, full of a lust she hadn't seen since she played water polo for GB schoolgirls. No one else would have noticed but her. Wives could tell. Just taken two decades to see the naked truth about her husband Harry Wade. He was and is a paedophile.

11: CHINA

There, she'd said it and it felt good. Made her feel giddy, forget herself for a nanosecond.

Kill Chip Mackie and Ged Grant.

Wow, Plan B by Dexys Midnight Runners leaps into her mind, Kevin Rowland pouring out his heart about always searching for something.

She wants Chip Mackie and Ged Grant dead.

Easy dream, less easy to do, unless your name is Jak and you murder with impunity. Forget Bill Withers, Kevin, and him being good for you. Jak would be good for her when Plan B replaced Plan A. That's your forfeit if I beat you at running, she said, which she knew she would. Another euphoric surge charges from the top of her neck to the bottom of her spine and beyond. The feeling was almost orgasmic and she has to pinch herself hard to stop them from multiplying. She needs to focus on Plan B. Identifying a new plan is not enough. It has to be successfully implemented too by winning the

heart and mind of her extraordinary White Stallion Man.
I am just a girl, an ordinary girl. You're bound to win, she
said.

Thought this place was bugged, said Jak, we were being
watched all the time by a criminal mastermind?

China stood hands on hips and felt the grin spread across
her face, hoping she did not look like she was gloating too
much.

The music had stopped.

Their voices could be heard. Would Chip be watching
right this second? Not likely. Didn't like to see her fucking.
Not now, not anymore. Besides, he had better things to do.
If he was watching her 24/7, how could he rescue Paradise
Hills from financial ruin. The property development was in
serious financial trouble and needed a serious cash injection.
That was Chris DeVeres' verdict when China quizzed him
over coffee and biscuits in Candy's World. Chip, or Denzil
more likely, would be permanently recording what was
happening. Rest assured he'd also be watching it in the
near future, fast forwarding with the slow motion option,
depending who was on the screen. How are you going to
do it, use your gun, she asked, picking up the cold steel
weapon from the table. The weapon in her palm made her
even giddier. Not sure how you're going to do it, but you'll
work out a way, said China, pushing for a response.

Jak smiled at her indulgently, how she envisaged a father
would patronise a small spoiled child used to getting its own
way. It's not going to happen, he said, there's no race for us
to run. No forfeits for us to fulfil. He walked slowly into
the kitchen, checked the timing on the washing machine.
Twenty minutes, he said, twenty five max to get dressed.
Then I'll be ready to go. Forget them silly instructions to
wait until it gets dark. Better call my taxi.

Please. Listen to me, said China, realising she has

seriously misjudged the mood. He'd shown tenderness. He'd been polite. He'd cared. He could save her. Her and Rose. He was her White Stallion Man. He was wearing White not Black CK boxers. He was on the side of good. What other signs did she need? She'd let her guard down. She threw the gun onto the leather sofa, unsure of her next move.

I've got money, she said: *money she'd set aside for a restaurant on a beach with the waves lapping at her feet.* I can pay you. What's your normal rate?

She said it in a whisper, pushing him to the floor by the washing machine, holding his head in her hands, looking deep into his Ice Cold Blue Eyes. Schizophrenic Eyes; Ice Cold Blue, Kind and Gentle, Armageddon Eyes. Eyes were the Windows to the Soul. Chip had dead eyes. Ged Grant the same. All the Merry Men shared the same dull eyed look from the excessive booze, speed and weed and whatever else they took during brutal 24 hour bonding sessions, only Denzil escaped the curse amongst Chip's gang. His were a startling green. Chris and Bing were different too, educated and cultured, bright eyed and intelligent. Poor Chris. Did he deserve to die because Chip and Ged allowed the dark fantasies inside his head to come alive? Did he deserve to die when others walk away scot free? There was no time to think, not until Plan B was done and dusted. Focus on one objective at a time or risk losing all in the confusion.

Please help me, China said to Jak. You're a good man. I can tell. I can feel it in your bones. Your flesh. Your soul. His hands reciprocate the touch, cup her face.

I am not an expert, he said, never profess to understand much about anything if I am being totally honest. But you're a young, attractive woman with the whole of your life ahead of you. You don't want to taint it. Not yours. Not your daughter's either. You don't want a killing on your conscience. Listen to the voice of experience.

Don't worry about my conscience, she replied. I'll live with it, happily.

You're better off legging it as fast as your pins can carry you and your daughter. Take her and the cash you've got stashed and run like the wind. Killing is never the answer to anything. Whatever you destroy always gets replaced, not often for the better. You hear what I am saying, he said.

How many people you killed, she asked.

Enough, he said.

What's two more, another two notches to your belt, she asked.

You're not listening. You can open that door and walk right out of Candy's World, whatever you call this place. I see what you've got here. If it's not you, it's somebody else. If you walk far away quick enough, he'll not chase you down, said Jak.

You don't know him like I do. He rages like a rabid dog. Rages at the moon. And everything that moves underneath it, said China.

Seems to me you're obsessed by him, said Jak, never going to pull that many strings if you move fast and far enough away, like I've just said. Not being funny but you're one of many. Girls like you grow on trees. And in my experience men don't like to chase too much. We're all dogs chasing cars. Once they pull away we stop and go back to licking our balls.

Says he loves me, said China, feeling sick at the thought, feeling the urge to move, to run, to jump, to swing through the air, to conjure up a mindfulness moment to dislodge the nightmare picture of his *love and lust*.

He'll get over you, said Jak, move onto his next cashcow.

Says he'll kill me if I ever betray him, said China.

All talk. Men like him are full of shit. Goes with the territory when they dress like clowns in golf clobber.

Even after you have just killed for him, she asked.

Not him. I kill for commerce, said Jak.

All talk? Look at my wrists, said China, removing the bangles and the bracelets she'd been so conscious of earlier. Now, for reasons beyond her comprehension, it seemed appropriate to shed a layer of skin or two.

Let him see the real her, the vulnerable her that needed a Knight on a White Charger Riding to the Rescue - or failing that a near-naked shooter with a gun. Plan B: Kevin singing about closed eyes, holding hands and together making a stand. Please, please make a stand for me Jak, my White Stallion Man.

Three faint white scars crisscross each of her wrists.

He did that to me, she said. Hit me, punched me and dragged me around the house by my hair. Not this wig. My real hair. Pulled so hard huge tufts came out. Plays Mr Cool until he snaps. Then he's the devil. Knocked me senseless, dragged me to the bathroom, ran the bath, held me in his arms. Cut my wrists, one then the other. Drew blood, let them bleed. Told me he'd accompany me to the other side. Make sure I crossed over nicely when I joined my mum and my silly boyfriend, both of them burning in hell.

Your daughter's father, Danny, the tattoo on your butt, he asked.

Yes. Poor sap, he wasn't even the father. Thought he was doing the right thing. I was three or four months pregnant. Bleeding on the floor concussed, my scrambled senses gradually returning, aware I was cut and getting weaker, unsure what was happening, whether I'd miscarried, pissed myself or simply disintegrated and was in the process of topping myself. I was vaguely aware of getting cold, really cold, shivering and trembling, suffering from hypothermia, unable to even recognise who Danny was or who he had been. I had no context while I was losing my grip on life.

Chip said if I was cold, he'd put me in the bath, that would warm me up, help the blood flow faster, drain my body quicker. I would pass easier. If I wanted to stay alive all I had to do was promise to be a good girl, an ordinary good girl who did as she was told and stopped making up silly, silly stories. All the time, he's stroking my hair, pulling it to keep me awake when I start drifting off. Telling me all I got to do is behave; otherwise what's the point of having me around if I cause grief and spread malicious lies and untruths, a silly girl crying wolf. Nobody would ever believe the words of an unbalanced teenage slut over a famous celebrity golfer who had almost won the Open and was a successful businessman to boot. I'd have gone if I hadn't had a tiny life inside me, dependent on me for everything. I believe I would have, honestly hand on my heart. I barely had the energy to summon any words. I managed OK, I'll do it but don't hurt Danny. He says it's too late to help him, although not too late to join him in an unmarked grave. But I need to say the words. So I do. Slowly. Because I am getting weaker and weaker. So I swear to stop making up stories. Swear to be good. Swear to tell nobody nothing that he won't like. Is that OK, I asked, my tears diluting my blood. Sure, he says, now show me you really, really love me. Then we'll get you sorted out.

China realised she was crying, head bowed deep into her chest, hands still holding his face, his hands clasping hers.

Plan A or Plan B forgotten about while she relived an attempted murder disguised as a bathroom suicide.

In the aftermath of the incident, she was sectioned for a month by Chip and had social services crawling all over her and her baby from that day onwards, looking for any excuse to take the child off her.

Ironically, only Chip stopped them from permanently

splitting up mother and daughter, vouching for her good behaviour.

She'd never told anyone that story or opened her heart to a stranger.

Only Danny knew, poor mixed-up orphan Danny, a dozen years older than her who believed he'd fathered her unborn child. Poor mixed-up lovestruck Danny, who had promised her the world. Said all you needed was a guitar and a few songs. Introduced her to Mott The Hoople, Dexys Midnight Runners, Lynyrd Skynyrd, and loads more ancient bands from way before she was born. Poor silly mixed up bastard Danny, don't believe the propaganda. Music only matters to people with souls. Bastards like Chip and Ged would always remain untouched by its powers.

You know dying in the bath with slashed wrists must be in my genes. My mother had done it too. My unknown mother, Marilyn McHale. The woman with no smell. No personality beyond old black and white photographs. I am my mother reincarnated. Her death is my death. They, whoever they are, say suicide runs in the family, daughters emulating mothers, sons copying fathers.

All the time she is speaking she knows if Chip is listening she is dead meat. She was dead meat anyway if he had ordered the killing of Chris.

Tying up loose ends was a habit of his.

Story over.

China was scared to look at the condemnation in Jak's Ice Cold Blue Eyes and avoided contact.

A hand lifted her chin. I am sorry, he said. It's not my problem. I've got to call Turner. Get my lift sorted out. I have enough worries of my own.

And he made the call.

It's Jak. Need to leave now. No waiting until it's dark. What's the address of this place?

She told him.

Post code too. 45 minutes.

A car would be outside. Beep three times, out the house and in the car.

She heard him repeat the instructions on the phone.

When he had finished, he moved away from her, walked through the kitchen, hand brushing the bottle of Jack gently, standing naked by one of the windows looking over the Paradise Hills golf course and beyond that the ocean, totally disinterested in her slashed wrists and the pain she has endured damn near most of her life.

The Ice Cold Blue Eyes of the White Stallion Man had lied to her.

Was there nothing left to believe in?

She'd bled her heart dry and he wasn't in the slightest bit interested.

What did it take to find a decent human being to care enough to shout out STOP.

This behaviour is not acceptable under any circumstances.

Why were so many able to turn the other cheek so easily?

Please God, if you exist, send someone to help me.

I want an interventionist God.

12: DEEKS

Harry Wade composes himself quickly, wipes the lust and the sweat from his face with a clean white hanky, blames dodgy air conditioning for the excessive heat in the office.

He presses his intercom and asks a colleague to arrange a patrol car to be out front in five minutes.

What are you doing, asked Deeks.

A lift home, you're in no fit state to drive yourself, he replied.

Why can't you drive? We can go home together?

I've got to stay here. Don't know what time I'm back. Sort my own food out, said Harry, inspecting the damp white cloth to avoid looking at her.

In normal circumstances Harry does good eye contact. She's seen him practising in the mirror, imitating Robert De Niro's Taxi Driver.

You're a witness like me, nothing you can add to the situation, said Deeks, scratching at the top Harry had given her, feeling uncomfortable, unsure whether it was because the shirt had been worn before or the cold realisation her husband was sexually turned on by Class 9 images of penetrative child abuse carried out by adults.

Whatever the reason, her skin felt like insects and bugs were crawling underneath it.

She was convinced it had not been her overactive imagination. She had seen his body, his face, his eyes. Seen the pores open, sweat instantly seep through. A large slow alien pulse in his neck throbbed several times. She had not been deceived.

Get me a coffee will you, please. And this top feels awful. Mind if I change it, asked Deeks, slipping it off and casually discarding it on the back of a chair, topless again.

When the sex had dried up she'd been convinced he was having an affair, despite never finding any evidence in the house or in his behaviour patterns at work or when they were out socialising. She'd looked, hard and often for the telltale signs. She was a good and thorough detective, discussed the generic subject of extra-marital affairs with female friends not in the force, almost come to the conclusion his age and the pressure of the job were to blame, leaving him uninterested in sex, drained of testosterone.

Until today.

Coffee Harry, my mouth feels like the inside of your kitbag, she said, searching the heavy-duty canvas bag for a clean top, shifting sports shoes, gels and strappings, unsure what she expects to find other than something unexpected, a gadget or a storage device to confirm his lust for sex with children.

She knows the way paedophiles operate, avidly collecting images and videos for later gratification.

Harry, her Harry, would be no different.

Sugar, milk, asked Harry. Shows you how far they had

grown apart without even knowing it. He cannot remember how she takes her coffee. How long had they been married?

Both, she said.

Back in a minute or two then, he replied, touching her bare shoulder as he leaves the office.

She flinches, feels disgusted at his touch, the insects recoiling under her skin in protest at his contact.

You OK, he asked, standing by the door.

For a moment he has washed away the years and is standing there, all gauche and thin, like he'd been when she fell head over heels and her concerns were his concerns and he'd stop at nothing to please her.

Just Cindy, silly Cindy, she replied, absently picking out and smelling an orange top.

It hadn't been worn.

There was nothing else of any interest in the bag.

She slips the top on, watches him stroll down the corridor and make a call on his mobile phone.

To be a fly on the wall of that conversation.

Who was he calling or warning?

She scans his office.

Nothing untoward jumps out at her.

No spare mobiles or external hard drives.

The draws are unlocked.

He appears to be operating in a secret-free zone on the surface but then paedophiles are very clever at covering their tracks.

Just like Chris DeVeres.

Where would Harry hide his stuff?

Harry is meticulous in the office and at home.

He folds his own clothes. Empties his own pockets before throwing things in the dirty laundry.

Irons his own tailor-made striped shirts for the week every Sunday.

Hand presses his collection of pink, purple and lilac silk ties.

Washes and hoovers and polishes his car every weekend.

His car.

His bloody car.

The obvious hiding place.

His pride and joy.

The coffee tastes like shit, he'd forgotten the sugar.

Hurry it up, there's a vehicle waiting at the front. They'll take you home, he said.

A waste of resources Harry. We can't tie up a patrol car driving me home. Not when we're hunting for a cop killer. You know how it will look, what people will say, she replied.

Where's yours, asked Harry, using the intercom to cancel the car.

In the city. Behind the hotel. Probably got a parking ticket too. Bastards. If you could get that rescinded, said Deeks, holding her hands out for the keys.

How do I get home, he asked.

You'll not be coming home to my house anytime soon buddy, said Deeks to herself, already planning ahead about who she would ask to search the car with her.

Somebody from the team as long as it wasn't Minty.

He could be seen to have a vested interest in bringing down Harry Wade and she wanted to play this one by the book.

13: CHIP

Tell me Chip, if you don't mind me calling you Chip, how did you get the name Chip, Chip, asked Anna Judd again, wiping her runny nose, checking the tape recorder is running.

He smiles a winning smile, sips strong black coffee, plays the question with a straight bat, offers her a sea-salted crisp from the gratis small bowl on the table. Why do you ask, he said.

I get the same sort of question myself on account of my boyfriend's name, Michael Truth, who just happens to be an investigative journalist. Imagine the Mickie taking we have to endure when we're out on the town or seeing my folks and their friends.

Mickie, Mackie, whatever, said Chip. The myth, girls, the story that is integral to the golf legend that is Chip Mackie.

I played at the Open as an amateur, 16 years old and wet

behind the ears, barely needed to shave but once a week. Still thought my John Thomas, huge as it was dangling between my legs, was for pissing through, better not print that snippet, but you get the picture. 16 years of age, my first major, had one of those rounds where you walk on water. I could not miss. Chipped in off the green four consecutive holes in the last six holes to shoot a 69. Saved five shots, each shot meant, each played to get close to the pin. The gods were shining down on me that day. Lowest amateur score that year, the silver medal. Never repeated the feat in all the years that followed, said Chip, shrugging his broad shoulders, such is life. They collectively laugh out loud, far more than the story merits; excessive coke does that to people. Chip wishes the dumb pain-in-the-butt interview could finish so he could locate bloody Eddie. The idiot was putting them all at risk. Harry Wade could not always be relied upon to dig them out of a hole as he'd done with Christian Big Mouth DeVeres. The accountant had called Bing, his client and so-called friend, to tell him about his predicament without going into specific details. Bing had told Chip because he correctly saw the Paradise Hills project was at risk. Chip had contacted Harry and told him they wanted a time and a public place to permanently take care of Chris DeVeres. They should have been watertight but weren't. It worried him. He didn't like plans being ignored. He didn't like deviation or false laughter. Didn't like the two girls with their high heels and make up and long legs and low cut blouses showing off too much mature bosom. He didn't like posh rich girls born with silver spoons thinking they were better than him. Their toff voices and shrill laughter really, really irritated him.

Lesson time for the two girls. Turns off the tape recorder. The actuality, girls, how good old Terry Mackie really earned the nickname Chip.

This isn't for print. When I was young I was a bit of a tearaway. Hung around with a bunch of kids, called ourselves the Merry Men after Robin Hood and the fact we were merrily pie-eyed most of the time. We were a bit wild, could have been in trouble with the law until golf saved me from myself and I saved them. We were all into boxing. We were told to keep our mouths shut when we sparred. No talking. No yapping because a tap on the jaw when it was flapping could easily crack and break it. One night we're out, having a few wets, a few laughs, chasing a bit of skirt, when we get to discussing if it's true about the tapping and the yapping and the snapping. I have a bet with my mate Ged. Tell him I think it is. He says no way. We're eating curried chips. Watch this, I tell him, watch this good. This kid is walking by, a drummer in a band we knew vaguely. I offer him a chip. Hey Paul, how you hanging? Paul takes it, opens his mouth to scoff it and I smack him as hard as I can, flush on his jaw. Boy, you could hear the crack right across the city. Ged was at him quick as a flash, bashing him on the top of the head like his nut was a tent pole, driving him into the ground. We were an awesome team. City boys, born and bred.

Sally swallows hard, the PR girl puts her hand on the journalist's, that's not for your piece Anna darling, just Chip's wicked sense of humour, that's golfers for you, winding you up. He's an old softy really. Definitely forget that anecdote, darling. Just need to go for a leak, she's right Anna. Just my wry sense of humour. I had a poor upbringing, had my fair share of tragedy, professional and personal, in my life. My wife tops herself. Leaves me with a family to bring up on my todd. I have a daughter who despises me for no apparent reason, who has tried to emulate her mother on several occasions. I've no time for mindless violence. It is not my style. Mindlessness never achieves anything. You always need a reason. Don't print that stuff about my daughter either. He saunters out of the clubhouse, annoyed that he had successfully wound himself up into a minor rage when there was no need. Worse, he was unsure if Anna Judd had been as shocked as he had expected. Sally was catching flies. But that Anna, that Anna didn't looked mithered one little bit, as if she had already heard the story before. His migraine was force 10 strength and his feelings of paranoia matched the hurricane intensity of his headache. The pills that he popped were useless. The more he took, the less impact they had. Tell the truth, the best remedy for his head would be to feed Eddie Doyle a large portion of fish and chips next time they met up, have the shithead sucking his food through a straw for the next six months.

Outside he surveys the championship golf course he has built, turning a desolate strip of sandy coastline into a potential goldmine, or a *golfmine*. Christ, he was beginning to think like Bing talked, all corporate ping pong pitter patter bullshit. Should have used golfmine to impress the writer woman, playing all nonchalant with him. Chip was under no illusions about his talents as a designer, a creator of landscapes. Yes, the track was pretty good but it was just a golf course. Golf was just a game. You could not live off a reputation as a good journeyman golfer once you lost your playing edge. You needed cash. Lots of it. Cash bought 'fuck off' freedom where you were beholden to no one. If you had enough, even the toffs had to sit up and take notice. He wanted that so much. Wanted their admiration and their fear in equal measure, same as how Turner seemed to inspire Bing. The upper class idiot spoke of Turner in revered terms and tiptoed around him in case he upset his sensibilities when it was his bloody pet monkey that had messed up. Damn Eddie. He should have stayed at Candy's World as instructed. How hard was it to follow simple directions. Harry could not run the same trick twice, delaying everyone while Chip organised another hit with Bing and Turner. The serious fraud squad would follow the money and bring them all down. Harry was a good sort, one of the boys. He was keeping him in the picture with the hunt. Told him they've not even identified Jimmy Doyle yet. Bloody cops couldn't catch a cold let alone criminals. Harry had laughed out loud at the chaotic response, cops chasing all over the city on wild goose chases as call after call fed through to 999 in the aftermath of the four year old's death. Not that his humour had stayed intact for long. Harry Wade had sounded pretty much on edge last time they spoke. He had said it was all under control, nothing to report. That had become I might have a problem with a colleague, who also happens to be my bloody wife, to I have got a fucking big problem, what am I going to do? A problem shared is a problem halved. More bullshit. Harry was passing decisions to Chip like everyone else. Chip couldn't anticipate domestics between husband and wife. Harry should just punch her lights out, hospitalise the bitch for a week or two. That would resolve the problem. On screen, China and the monkey were rutting like rabbits as if God had announced imminent world destruction, rubbing his nose in it with their carnal lust. Time for one last bang before we explode. The two of them plotting rebellion. Thinking they could outwit him, cheat him of what was rightfully his. He'd have the last laugh. Power of attorney papers for Rose's guardianship were already drawn up to make it all legal, whenever he wanted to push the button. China's Will passed all the businesses she 'owned' into a trust fund for Rose, which Chip would administer until the child came of age. China didn't even know she had written one. His trump card had been the social workers. They were willing him to section her again, offering fostering rather than adoption as his carrot. Now he had other options. The power was all his. Fuck them, now was the time. Ged and Denzil would be here with the merchandise. The Khans would collect and cough up the cash injection that would give him almost equal shares in Paradise. Then he could really start achieving things. Without Bing holding him back. Slowing down the decisions making. All that was needed was a few obstacles to be cleared out of the way.

Switchblade Eddie answers second ring. Where are you, asked Chip. Silence. Sobbing. Chip tries again. Eddie. Where are you? You near Candy's World?

He's dead, Chip, bloody Jimmy's dead. All my fault. My bloody fault, weeped Eddie.

No, Eddie, not yours. China and Turner's monkey have been laughing out loud. Been watching them. Taking the piss out of you and your brother. I feel disgusted. Sick at what I am hearing. Laughing at you and your Jimmy, can you hear me Eddie? Both of them showing you and Jimmy no respect. Don't let them get away with it, said Chip.

I am wrecked Chip. I need to sleep. I need..., sobbed Eddie.

Revenge is what you need. For your brother. That coward pushed your brother right into the bus. Poor sod had no chance. Harry Wade told me direct. No word of a lie. Straight from the horse's mouth. You go and sort them out. Do them both with your switchblade Eddie. Messy as you like, said Chip.

The fucking grease monkey will be a pleasure. Never liked him. All mouth, no trousers, said Eddie.

Do him quick, Eddie.

China?

Her too.

You sure, asked Eddie.

Chip paused for a second, considered the situation fully.

She's told him the bathroom story. If she hadn't she would soon. He could tell. She had that look of belligerence about her, even on the small mobile screen. Even the way she was fucking with such uninhibited abandon was sticking two fingers up at him. The bathroom stories would lead to stories about other rooms. The Girl Who Cried Wolf had reached her finite shelf life. Maybe the painkillers were warping his mind. The stress of it all blurring his tunnel vision. Too many balls in the air to juggle for any one man. Maybe... No, it was always inevitable. She was wilful like her mother, too wilful, had too many dark secrets to reveal that others might one day believe. Then the whole plan was kaput leaving him a busted flush, yesterday's news, the golfer who blew the Open, a failure on and off the course. That was not going to happen. Sure I am sure, said Chip. Do her once you've got rid of Turner's ape. Hit him hard. Hit him with all you've got. He's dangerous. A wounded animal can still bite if you don't hit him hard.

China? She's your....

Not anymore. Hasn't been for a long time. Too much like her mother. We'll be doing her a favour long term. Putting her out of her misery. If she was a dog, we wouldn't hesitate, said Chip.

Shall we wait for Ged, asked Eddie.

You're joking Eddie. You're the man. I should have listened to you in the first place. Never brought in an outsider. If you put it right, I'll be grateful. Ged too. We'll see you right, gift you a Paradise Hills lodge, you'll have a secure income for life, said Chip.

OK, I am reading you right. Reading you clear Big Man. Afterwards, asked Eddie.

We'll have a booze. Ged will help you clear up. Don't spare the rod. You hear me?

Chip cut the connection. Felt a lot better. Action taken.

A problem resolved. Turner and Bing would never need to know. He didn't want Ged and Denzil being distracted when they got here because those Asians were tricky fat bastards, giving themselves bloody English first names as if that integrated them, twats with ideas above their station. He checked his mobile yet again, took one last look at China with Turner's idiot deep in conversation. He was right. Both had to be executed. Turned to go back to finish the interview and almost knocked over Bing standing right behind him.

Turner wants a word, said Bing.

Where is he, asked Chip. Bing pointed to the sky. A helicopter was descending. Chip had been too distracted to notice. Did you hear any of that conversation, asked Chip.

No, said Bing, I never hear or see anything, rude to eavesdrop. I'll go and talk to the cute sexy journalist, think she fancies her little Bing Boy. Good luck with Turner.

Why is he here, asked Chip.

Who knows, said Bing.

To see me?

Chip pops another two pills as the chopper circles and lands. Paul the drummer had almost died after his beating, was in intensive care for a week. Never the same afterwards. He stopped playing his music, moved away from the city. They'd never been prosecuted. Uniformed police turned up and him and Ged lied through their back teeth. A young beat bobby called Harry Wade swallowed their story hook, line and sinker. They bunged him a ton a week later and had a few wets, the start of a long mutually beneficial relationship for the three of them. Some punchlines you kept to yourself. Shame he would have loved to tell them he owned the law in the city. Would be good if they knew. They'd be so terrified of him. He'd be untouchable. To be honest, he was pretty close now. Just needed to finish the tidying.

14: DEEKS

Deeks picks Ed Boucher to help search Harry Wade's car. She literally bursts into the office, almost losing her footing in her rush. Ed with me, now, we'll be off site for an hour or so, incommunicado.

They walk towards the car park at a fast pace. Boucher, three inches shorter than Deeks and nowhere near as fit, struggles to keep up.

What are we planning on doing Ma'am, thought we were restricted on account of us having seen Cindy, you know? They've identified the knob on the bike, the one who was decapitated. Jimmy Doyle. Local hard nut not on our radar as a sex pest. Violence. Robbery. No fiddling, said Boucher.

She ignores him. Jimmy fucking Doyle is right down the pecking of her priorities. She has bigger fish to catch, namely her husband Harry Wade and whoever else fiddled in his paedophile gang. Passenger side.

I'll drive, she said, strapping herself in, conscious she is braless when the seat belt dissects her small boobs. She can feel the heat emanating from Boucher's body. He's avoiding visual contact. Eyes looking out the passenger window. His side of the windscreen all steamed up. Wants to ask about progress with Chris but leaves the questions unasked. They stop at a petrol station fives minutes from the office. She parks under a lone street light away from drivers refuelling and pedestrians shopping for essentials. The two of them sit in silence, waiting. Deeks is unsure why she's immobile. The task is obvious. Search the car for storage hard drives or mobile devices. They've done it loads of times before. They know where to look. There are not that many places to hide things in a car. All she has to do is brief Boucher why they are checking a senior police officer's car who also happens to be her husband. Explain why she is suspicious. An officer's intuition, a woman's, a wife's. It all made perfect sense staring Harry down in the office with an involuntarily bulging muscle spasm threatening to burst out of his neck.

Seeing his reaction to the images.

So what was stopping her?

You know I am flattered that you're interested in me, said Boucher, I really am. You're a very sexy woman and very attractive and I certainly don't see a problem with our age difference or the fact you're my boss. But with all due respect, Cindy's not even cold in the mortuary. I know it relieves tension. Sex does that. Distracts you from the pain of a major bereavement. Also to be honest, it's no secret amongst the team that you and Minty have your 'thing'. I have no qualms about what two married people do, I am not one to pass moral judgement on consenting adults, like you say about Lenny Bruce, one or nine adults, that's fine and dandy, with me too. Minty praises you for your energy and enthusiasm and your imagination but role playing and role reversals - both would make me feel very uncomfortable, even as an experiment. I am not a prude by any means and I think I am more liberal than a lot of my peers.

What's he banging on about?

She's aware that Boucher, the normally taciturn detective, is having an attack of the verbals. Cindy. Sex. Minty. Consent. Role fucking reversals?

She's trying to compute what to do, how to handle a delicate and difficult situation and doesn't need his verbal bollocks burbling in her ears.

Like I said, I am flattered that you've picked me, but to be perfectly frank, this is not my cup of tea, continued Boucher relentlessly. Please don't take it the wrong way. Or let my rejection of your advances spoil our working relationship, dare I say our personal friendship. I would need to take things a lot slower than 'getting to it' in a car, especially your husband's, without us getting to know each other first. We would have to build up towards it...have lunch a couple of times, perhaps dinner, a show...

Boucher shut the fuck up. Let me think, said Deeks.

His endless rant had disrupted her flow. She's always thought Minty was discreet rather than a braggart. If Boucher and the office knew, then the entire building would be in on the secret. Harry would be well aware of what was going down too. Never said a word or challenged her behaviour. Her banging a colleague meant sweet FA to him. She knew why. Just find the evidence in the car. Let Boucher corroborate the find.

Purely from a work perspective, it's not good for moral if you're sleeping with half the team, suggested Boucher, as you would be now that Cindy has departed; it might create friction amongst other members. They may perceive you favouring Minty, giving him preferential treatment, me too. When it comes to promotions and references and the like.

Still rattling on. The man was an idiot, wet and inept

and sexually unaware, an incompetent. She'd replace him soon as she could. Minty too, ship them both out to pastures new to fantasise and boast. Once the fall out from Harry's exposure and disgrace had dispersed.

She leaned towards the glove compartment, felt Boucher twitch, hands covering his groin, unsure how she stopped herself from howling with laughter. She felt like clipping him around the ear, tell him to man up. Instead, she flips the catch and looks inside. Business cards, power leads for his mobile, a Swiss army penknife and a Mars Bar to help him work, rest and play with himself over Class 9 images.

There would be considerable consequences from Harry's unveiling as a paedophile. They'd be pointing the finger at her too. How come she didn't know. She must have known. Bet they were both deviants. Her with a strap drilling one of her own male colleagues. Not normal. No Sir, not normal at all. Tarred with Harry's brush, career down the pan like his. She checked the armrest between the seats, flipped it up. Spotless. OCD Harry. Flipped the sunshields. A couple more business cards sticking out.

What are you looking for Maam? I've tried to explain, said Boucher.

Get out, get out now. Leave me alone, Deeks snapped.

Boucher was out faster than at anytime he'd moved in the two years he'd worked with the sex crime team.

She watched him scuttle off in the wing mirror, fat arse waddling in his urgency to run from his MILF cougar boss. How soon before her attempted mythological seduction would become fact?

He'd be on his mobile as soon as he was out of her eyesight, flaming her humiliation.

Where was it written that a lonely, unloved woman could not find solace in a physical relationship without it being perceived as dirty and sordid? Men could do anything and it was cool, a woman playing by the same rules was a slag, a slut, a sexual deviant.

She swallowed hard, tasted the sick at the back of her throat, the tears running down her face, the floodgates open again as she silently sobs for Cindy and herself. She imagined herself sobbing at the funeral, the older aunt's role to be a rock for all of Cindy's friends. The wild girl who stunned everyone with a spectacular pole dancing display, said she'd learned a special routine just for Cindy to celebrate her big day. Cindy her new best friend.

Deeks wondered if she knew yet that her new best friend was dead. She could not remember her name, only that she was tall and in great shape.

Made her envious of her obvious youth.

Hoped she was single and didn't have to live with the disappointment of discovering husbands and lovers would always let her down. Deeks adjusted the rear view mirror to see the mascara trails running down her face.

Fuck Harry for doing this to her.

Children were the innocents. The duty of care of all adults was to protect them, give them a fair and equal chance of happiness and a proper start in life.

Not too much to ask. Fucking Harry.

She started the car, put it into reverse, was about to adjust the rear view, saw only red eyes staring back at her. Fuck you Harry. Fuck you Christian DeVeres. Fuck you all. She killed the engine.

Put on the hand brake.

Reached into the glove compartment.

Pulled out the Swiss Army Knife. Squeezed it tight in her hand.

Where shall we start Cindy? Where shall we fucking start?

15: JAK

Forty five minutes and he'd removed from the scene of the crime, never to return, said Turner.

In 24 hours Jak would be on a beach bronzing gently, scoffing fresh sea food and reading Andy McNab or Chris Ryan or whatever soldier writers floated his boat although Turner personally prefers British writers like Boyd, Barnes and Banks. Turner told him the only thing on his mind would be sex, sea, sand and more sex. He'd love to meet up, chew the fat, except any association was a potential banana skin for them both. If Jak was ever busted, Turner would be better placed to work the shadows, helping his 'second son' from the dark recesses of the corridors of power. They'd touch base again in 24 hours.

Typical Turner banter.

All he has to do is confirm the lift. Give Jak's ears a break from the bashing.

Turner could and did chunter and bluster for Middle England.

The coupling was no different to his early days in the services, banging like sewer rats when they weren't fighting, drinking or killing.

He'd not changed one bit, still as callous as he had been then.

No wonder he could never form long term relationships with women.

Not his fault.

Just as the four year old was not his fault or the kid herding goats.

The girl with no name wanting him to murder Chip and his sidekick Ged Grant.

What an insane idea, totally radio rental. Earn him life for starters if he's caught without Turner's protection. Despite the ludicrous nature of the suggestion, he should let her down as gently as he could, although he was not sure how, without appearing too stark. If he asked her for her name now it might indicate he cares, give her false hope when there was none. He's away in forty five minutes, less now, probably forty.

She's busy stirring, first the chilli, then the bolognese, red-eyed and humming to herself.

The tune she'd played earlier, the Wicked Game, the theme for a television series or was it a film. He vaguely remembered a video with a super model and the handsome sexy singer mucking about in the surf on the west coast of America. That would be him soon in 24 hours. Messing in the waves, minus the supermodel in his arms mind. He'd probably have to buy the company in cash or in kind as usual.

You could take me with you, me and my daughter, said China. We can go, me, you and Rose and we can travel light. I've got cash and passports. Just collect her from Paradise Hills. Soon as we're out of the country, we'll leave you alone, take our chances on our own.

He laughs. We've discussed this before. There is nothing stopping you walking out the door now. You don't need me, he said, laughing.

Leave me the gun. I'll do it myself. I'll buy it off you. Whatever you want, she said.

He laughs again, as if he'd leave the evidence that could earn him a life sentence. Wasn't his to sell anyway. The idiots had hired it.

What was so funny, she asked, what was so amusing. I want to be normal. I want to be clean and look in the mirror and like what I see. I want Rose to live a life that's not mine. You know it's not my fault. Never was. How silly of me to have expectations to even think that a man who could kill a child would have compassion enough to help another human being. You kill a four year old and don't bat an eyelid.

Not her fault.

A familiar refrain. She's echoing him, reading his mind with her telepathic powers. They have empathy. No they don't. He glances at the tumble dryer, checking how long it will take before he can get dressed, wanting her to shut up about the bloody four year old.

Not his fault.
He was not to blame.

I am not judging you, who am I to judge anyone, she said. Just saw compassion and understanding writ in large

95

CAPITAL LETTERS across your face. Thought I meant something to you.

In a couple of a hours? Dream on. Love took weeks, months. Not a quick bunk up, he said.

You can fall in love in a lot less. You're my White Stallion Man come to save me and Rose, said China.

White Stallion what? Sex is sex, nothing more. You sell sex. Death is my product. I need to unload afterwards and you were on hand, he said, looking at her stirring the chilli, tears running unchecked down her face.

He wanted to tell her to stop crying but there was no point when he was the cause.

Not my fault. Not your fault.

Life moves on. Nothing stays the same. And it changes yet again in 38 odd minutes, he said.

There's not an ounce of compassion in you. Don't you feel bad fucking someone young enough to be your daughter? Twice. You kill, you fuck and then you run like the coward you are, gutless and yellow to the core.

She might have had a point but she should keep it to herself. If she was a bloke, he'd have punched her lights out. Knocked her unconscious.

So he hits her with words.

I know what I am, he said. I know what you are too. A slapper, a tart, a whore, selling your body for peanuts. All the time your daughter is infected by your shameful mortality. Wipe your crocodile tears away.

Morality is the right word. You deal with mortality because you kill four year olds, she said.

Sticks and stones from a sex worker, he said.

Do you know how pompous you sound, judging me? My crocodile tears, she said.

Your child will judge you. Not me, he said.

You're right. She will. I am bad and I am evil. I am cursed. I deserve all that has and will come my way. But Rose doesn't. Why does she have to be punished? Why? What has she ever done to hurt anybody, she asked.

Jak wished he'd never said any of the words.

They'd spilled from his mouth before he could rein them in. Angry words that should have been directed at himself.

He knew how desperately he wanted a drink to black out the child in the city who was no different from the child in the mountain.

One minute herding goats. The next lying in the dust with his half head missing.

She'd done nothing to deserve the verbal beasting.

Sorry. I've seen a lot. Too much, he said.

When did you first kill someone, she asked. She was at it again, winding him up.

His sorrow was wasted on her.

At the age of 17, he said. He could not stop himself or the urge to retaliate, belittle and cheapen her with his hurtful words.

When did you have your first fuck?

Six.

Six what. Sixteen, he asked dismissively.

Six. Same age Rose will be in two months time, she said.

Fucking at six. Fuck off, you're a bloody lying fraud.

16: JAK

Six not sixteen.

Not his fault.
Not her fault.

Then who was to blame?

Jak was lost for words.

Six not sixteen.

17: CHINA

How dare you call me a whore? How dare you call me anything. You, you're a murderer. Killed a boy of four. And you're calling me. China explodes, the anger boils over uncontrolled. Nails dig hard into her arms, one punctures skin, draws blood.

She upends the pots of chilli and bolognese, sends them crashing to the floor.

She spots the gun and grabs it.

Aims it at Jak's groin. Shall I blow your cock into the stratosphere, render you impotent so you know how I feel? Lifts it slightly, aims at his heart. Can a bullet penetrate granite? Will it ricochet and kill another innocent four year old? Goes higher, aims at his head. I would you know. I fucking really would! How would you like it, she cried, exhaustion sapping the red mist.

Your finger is outside the trigger guard. You've had your flash of anger, said Jak. Let's have a reality check. It's not in your DNA to kill. Never has been and never will.

She looks at him. Think your DNA is different, she said. Having a gun pointed at you does not seem to worry you. I could be a waitress asking if you want a side salad with your main meal for all you care.

Jak holds out his hand for the gun. You don't need to deal with it this way, he said. I am sorry I spoke to you in that way. It was churlish.

Six not sixteen, she said, six not sixteen. Her voice as broken as her spirit. Six not sixteen. My own father. Chip.

Give me the gun, he said, walking towards her.

She puts the gun to her head. The end of the barrel pressing into the side of her skull. Finger on the trigger this time. Almost pressing. So easy. A fraction of an inch ends it all. Eyes shut tight. Face scrunched up. Oblivion beckons. Chasing stardust. Amongst the planets. Bliss. No more pain. No more suffering. No more anxiety. Her purgatory consigned to history, just another daft mad woman took another way out rather than wade through endless fields of wheat. *Stop the rock, this expired meat and bones package wants to get off.* She pictures it, her demise, the bullet travelling through her head with the greatest of ease, adding to the mess on the floor. When Chip was teaching her golf he always said visualise the end result. She was good at that. At picturing the end result. Which is why she knows the gun barrel pressed hard into her temple is for show, knowing that the character she plays has to be real if he is to believe her. It's a careful balancing act, mind. Get it wrong and she herself will be unable to judge reality from insanity. If that moment comes she'd be too far gone to pull herself back. That's the risk of playing wicked games when she's flaming the fires. Another time and another place she'd expect a blow to the head. A beating. Punches to punish her for threatening suicide. For being a pain. Her eyes are still closed. Waiting. Anticipating. Ready to ride the fists and the feet and the head butts. Men have always beaten on her or raped her or abused her. Taken what they wanted and cast her aside, apart from Chris. He'd been besotted, treated her gently, as if it was a love affair and not rape and sexual assault, thinking Rose was possibly his when China had dreamed up Plan A after watching hysterical news reports about prolific perverted celebrities interfering with young girls.

Jak's hand gently touches hers, moves the gun away from her head and down to her side.

Slowly he loosens her grip on the handle. Removes it from her grasp.

You never took the safety catch off, he said.

He leads her to the settee. Sits her down. Sits beside her. Holds her tight. In silence. She waits for him to speak but he says nothing. I am too tired to run in the quicksand by myself and carry a child with me, she said. I've been running on the spot all my life and getting nowhere. Is she speaking aloud or merely imagining herself saying the words to a man she barely knows, who earlier today has killed four people for money, a White Stallion Man holding her tight and then letting her go.

She opens her eyes.

Watches him go to the spin dryer.

Take out his clothes, shakes them into shape. He pulls on the top slowly, the grazes clearly painful despite his best efforts to pretend otherwise. He steps into the black jeans, brushes out a few more creases. He's going to help her, she can tell. It's a woman's intuition. They've connected. Even in the short time they've known each other. They've bonded. You'll like Rose, she said, looking at the photographs that adorn the open plan sitting area, remembering to take them with her if she has the time. He checks his watch. She never noticed he was wearing one. An ordinary watch. Nothing ostentatious or over the top. Not like Chip and his Merry Men with their outsized gangster gadgets dangling from fat tattooed limbs. We'll do it your way, she said. Just run. If we go now, together, we can make a clean break. You might be right. He won't chase me or Rose. We'll have to get her. Go to the Paradise Hills resort hotel. I've got our passports and money. Cash not cards or anything that can be traced. I'll get them. We'll travel light. He avoids the merging lakes of chilli, bolognese and Jack Daniels spreading across the marble floor.

I'll need to go upstairs, she said. Get changed. Need some clothes for Rose. We'll have to get her first. She's in room 203 at Paradise Hills. Jenny will be looking after her. Chip and his chaps will be drinking in the bar. Smash and grab raid. Karl might be with Jenny. He's no contest against you. One stare and he'll wee himself. Same with Denzil, if he's there. He's a tech geek. Lives in a vacuum, bloody autistic I reckon, Aspergers, whatever they call it. Only Ged is dangerous. We have to be careful with him. I am excited, Jak, very excited.

All the time Jak is mute. Slips on his jacket. Checks the pistol. Slips it inside his jacket.

She smiles. Wants to kiss him. Jak's continued silence says everything. Doesn't want to get sentimental when they are racing against the clock. Jeans and a white top and a leather jacket will do. Same look as his. Blend into the crowd. She can buy new for everything else. A totally clean break from Candy's World and the city that had nearly destroyed her.

Five minutes for me to get ready, she said, taking long quick strides to the staircase. She'll get dressed first. Collect a few things for Rose. Take the passports and the cash from their hiding place in her en suite toilet, the only place Denzil

Grant had guaranteed they'd not place a camera behind a mirror.

She said five but she wants to do it in less. Every minute counts. From upstairs, she hears a car horn beeps outside. Has 45 minutes passed that quickly? Time flies when you're having fun.

She hears the chain on the front door and the locks undone.

One minute, she shouts, hoping the sound travels through the house without getting lost in Candy's World's massive open spaces.

I am ready, she shouted again, running downstairs, two steps at a time, careful not to fall flat on her butt. That would be foolish.

The front door is wide open.

He's gone.

She steps outside.

Looks up the street.

A black car is turning left at the end of her road, left indicator flashing.

Back inside she sinks to the floor.

She was mad. Insane. A fantasist. Plan A fucked. Plan B fucked. China fucked. Everything fucked. Exhausted, she loses track of time.

A noise brings her out of her stupor.

He's come back to get her.

The White Stallion Man in all his Infinite Glory.

Except it's not.

Where's the cunt, demanded Switchblade Eddie?

18: DEEKS

She wanted to yell out loud Cindy, I've found it. I've found it.

Except she hadn't.

The car was a mess. All four doors open. Panels unscrewed and discarded. Passers by gave her a wide berth as she manically searched the vehicle and chatted incessantly to Cindy's ghost. Deeks wants to find an external hard drive in the car more than anything else in the world. She wants leverage to squeeze Harry. Knowing is no good, she needs hard evidence for a judge and a jury to convict. She prays silently to her God: *please, just give me a square black box no bigger than a holiday potboiler paperback. Please. For Cindy's sake.*

What you looking for missus, asked a young kid wearing a hoodie and holding a mountain bike.

Deeks glances behind, sees him staring at her bum

sticking out of the car. She reaches for the pepper spray in her handbag to incapacitate the rat boy. The spray is her best friend at a time like this; induces coughing, choking, nausea, temporary blindness and intense burning. It fucks people up good and proper. Cindy should have had some earlier this morning.

The boy flips the hood from his head, he's hardly into his teens.

Can I help you, lost your car keys, he asked.

My mind, I've lost my mind, said Deeks.

I can start it for you if you want, said the child, my first name is Darius but everyone calls me Sonny.

Keys are here, Sonny. What I am after is a little black box. Unfortunately it's not here.

I've got one, a little black box, said Sonny, delving into his coat and bringing out a battered old handheld cassette recorder.

What's that, she asked.

Dunno. Found it on the tip. But it's mine. Thrown away like, said Sonny, putting it back under his coat. Nobody owns it but Sonny.

How much, asked Deeks.

A delighted Sonny cycles off with his winnings.

Deeks holds the bagged up 'evidence' in her hands. Shrugs, as she imagines Cindy's horror at the blatant rule breaking. Exceptional circumstances, Cindy, exceptional circumstances. We've got a king to catch although the excitement of the chase is tempered by the realisation that her life will never be the same. Her sons will have to adjust to their changed circumstances.

She has seen it hundreds of times before, when they had swooped on paedophiles and arrested them. The look of total shock on the faces of the families and friends exposed to the Big Lie of a Loved One for the First Time. Her turn now. Nigel, Colin and Henry would understand. They were good boys, her boys, her genes, not his, her nurture, not his. He just gave them his name. Maybe they would take hers when Harry was locked away. She would not pressure them. They could decide themselves. She dreaded telling them. They'd understand when she explained why she did it. It was not everyday a wife lost a close colleague, a true friend, and discovered her husband was a paedophile. The ends justified the means: it is what I need to do Cindy, what I need to do for you. What now though? Let us get the bastards. That's what Cindy would have said if she hadn't jumped in front of an assassin's bullet. Harry Wade, your time is up.

She marches into the office.

The team beavering away, eyes glued to computer screens. Boucher head down. Minty head down. The other two heads down. They all know. The non-seduction already 'fact'.

Minty speaks. They want somebody to formally ID Cindy. Her family aren't local, other side of the country. We thought…one of us could do it if you weren't up to it.

Deeks clutches the evidence bag in her hand.

What have you got there, asked Ash.

Nothing important, Deeks replied, lying, knowing she was sailing close to the wind, her own head on the chopping block. Turfing Boucher out while she searched the car was only going to be interpreted one way.

Silly mistake.

Harry being Harry would fight for all he was worth. If he got a sniff of a procedural lapse, he'd smash a sledgehammer through their case. Tell me what's new, the highlights only chaps. We're on a schedule. His computers?

Ash stood up. A bit weird Boss. Some folders are cleverly encrypted. Going to take us a lot of time to access them. Others are not protected at all.

Maybe he didn't have time to archive, she said. What's on them?

Awful but not shocking, said Ash. All downloaded the last month, which equates with your 'no' time theory.

Anything else, she asked.

Dobbo stands as Ash sits.

I've matched his diary with the contact times with AprilShowers, said Dobbo. Same place every single time. A mansion out by Paradise Hills.

Called, she asked.

Candy's World, said Dobbo.

Who owns it?

Not sure. Managed by a finance company in Jersey. No other details yet, said Dobbo.

You asked them?

It's Sunday Boss. Even the cops on duty are on the beach.

Who lives there now?

Four people. Two adults. Two children. First, we've got China Mackie and her daughter, replied Dobbo. And two Americans, Coni McHale and Scarlett McHale. The former is a student, visa and everything else in order.

Who is China, asked Deeks.

An adult movie producer according to Google, said Dobbo. Just a kid. Father is Chip Mackie, the golfer who bottled the Open all those years ago. Blew the championship when it was literally in his pocket.

What's he do now, asked Deeks.

He's a property developer at the Paradise Hills resort with good old Hughie Bingham, our city's beloved Mr Charity. The man Chris called after we arrested him.

What are the relevant connections?

He's Chris's oldest client. Goes back two decades and more. Not far fetched that he would call. Bingham called the family solicitor, who called us, said Dobbo.

Did they meet, asked Deeks.

No time. Just furious phone calls, said Ash, interrupting. Anything on Bingham or Mackie?

Not a dicky, Harry will know them better than us, he plays golf there. He gets a complimentary membership, lucky bugger, so he is likely to know either or both, said Minty, doing little to hide his contempt for the implication Harry was having his palms greased at the Paradise Hills resort. Brilliant gym and outdoor pool but you would know all about that.

I wouldn't know. I use the municipal, said Deeks, who didn't know about the golf freebie. Harry kept that a secret. She never knew Harry was close with Bingham or Mackie either, celebrities in a northern city that was more like a village community. Never met the latter socially. Didn't like Minty's implication that she benefited from a freebie. What about the financials?

Complicated. Very complicated. Although it appears DeVeres recently started paying China two grand a month, six months ago, said Ash.

Wages from her old man, she asked.

From his personal account, Ash said. He's also set up a very complicated trust fund for the child on behalf of Chip Mackie.

China or Rose?

The latter.

Keep digging, said Deeks, pleased with their work. You're all doing great all of you. Tell them I'll go in 15 minutes, after I've spoken to Harry.

Upstairs on the senior management's corridor, she

enters without knocking. Harry is huddled over a map of the city with two serious crime detectives she recognises and despises, chubby cynical Billy Ginn and a graduate whippersnapper Gerry Pitt, Harry's right hand boys, brown nosing their way up the greasy pole in her husband's wake. They'd not been at the shooting. Must have come in when they heard about Cindy. Lots did when an officer was down. They all stand guiltily to attention when she enters, schoolboys caught smoking in the dorm.

We're in conference, said Harry, come back in a bit.

No, she said.

Don't worry, we'll go, said Ginn, the senior of the two detectives.

Stay, said Harry, it's not urgent. This is more important. Harry tells her that was embarrassing and not to do it again once Ginn and Pitt have left.

If that's embarrassing, what is this, she said, sliding the bagged and tagged imaginary hard drive towards the middle of the conference table.

No idea what you're on about love, said Harry, making no attempt to reach out and inspect the package. He'd stonewall as much as he could. Harry was good at stonewalling.

What's on it, she asked.

Never seen it before in my life, he replied.

Funny, I found it in your car, hidden. Looks like an external hard drive to me Harry. Where you store data, pictures, videos. What's on it Harry?

Harry remains motionless, arms folded defensively, slightly bristling with moral indignation but not wholly committed to the denial.

She can see he's thinking and assessing, working out the damage limitation permutations.

Trying to remember.

There was doubt. Harry's smart. Harry can think on his

feet quickly. Harry didn't get where he was today by being backwards coming forwards.

What are you trying to imply Sophie, he asked. I've never seen this before, no matter where you claim you've found it. Your word against mine. Careful we don't start digging our respective trenches so deep we're swallowing mouthfuls of mud for the rest of our born naturals.

Fingerprints will probably prove you're lying Harry, she said, leaning forward, revelling in his clear unease.

Who have you told, he asked, biting back, playing his joker card and coming up trumps.

There's the fucking rub, she knows, the bloody fucking cunting rub, as Hamlet would have said in the 21st Century.

She's told no one. Shared the information with no one because the info is only based on her intuition.

Harry could pick up on a vibe pretty fast. Contrary to gossip spread by jealous laggards, fools rarely got promoted beyond their abilities. You would underestimate Harry Wade at your peril. Sat there, arms folded, defensive, dangerous, a cornered animal waiting to counter attack, teeth sharpened, claws ready to rip her story to pieces if she slips up in the slightest.

You've not told anyone have you, he said, a wry smile breaks on his face as he sees a glimmer of light at the end of the pitch black tunnel.

She could lie to him and say she had but that would only further compromise the case against him if it ever got to that stage.

Judges and juries don't like the disingenuous collection and collation of evidence.

What will we find on the hard drive Harry? Will it shock us to the core, like those Grade 9 images of children with penetrative adults that you saw earlier? Worse? Believe me, there are worse images. Hard to imagine. Even you would be shocked, however sick you are Harry Wade. Unless there are worse images than I've ever seen on this hard drive. Is that it Harry? Is there? You can tell me straight. We can do a deal. I owe you that chance. Give us your friends, others who abuse children. You'll feel better, relieved of all the lies, the deceit, the pressure off your conscience.

Harry unfolds his arms, stands up and goes to pick up the evidence bag, his name on the packaging, today's date, her signature, no countersignature, yet.

She grabs it before he can.

He's uncertain.

Cannot remember.

Cannot be sure.

If he didn't leave it there, somebody else might have done. It happens.

Pragmatic Harry walks over to the window that overlooks the city that she knows he has policed all his working life. His city. His patch. His fiefdom as he often reminds her.

What do you want most of all, beyond all the co-operation bullshit you're spewing up, he asked her reflection in the window.

I want Cindy's killer, she said, remembering the casual assassin moments after killing Cindy, those ice cold light blue eyes meeting hers, admiring his handy work, before replacing his visor, so confident he would get away with the slaughter of innocents.

Sure, said Harry. I'll give you Cindy's killers if that gets you off my bloody back. Not that I am confessing to anything.

19: CHIP

Chip watches the sky blue helicopter circle above the resort, hovering over the 18th hole and the practice putting green.

He's not alone, a small crowd has joined him to see if anyone famous is arriving in the fancy transport.

On the periphery of the gathering he sees Rose with Jenny, the two of them have a bond and he's immediately envious. China has kept him away from his own granddaughter too long. China is or was a wilful spiteful girl, the spit of her late weak evil mother, even has her big brown green eyes. He was away playing golf in Spain the night his very drunk teetotal wife finally cut her wrists open in the bath, China asleep in the bedroom next to the bathroom. Sadly for the late Mrs Chip Mackie, Ged Grant wasn't kipping. A good lad Ged, salt of the earth. Never said much when he was sober because he knew actions spoke louder than words. Wetted he was as loud and boisterous as the others.

He glances up at the expensive flying machine, probably wouldn't get much change out of a quarter of a million just to park it in your back garden, let alone fly it. The world's greatest golfers, those with multiple slams and sponsorship deals with global brands, could buy themselves toys that cost the same as a couple of the lodges they were hawking at Paradise Hills.

He'd missed the boat with that eight iron all those years ago.

One shot.

One error.

Still rankled. Must have cost him the best part of ten or twenty million, possibly even more.

One bloody golf shot.

If the Good Lord gave him his time over again, the only thing he'd change was the club selection, a seven rather than an eight.

An area not far from the 18th is Bing's designated landing point for helicopters, marked with a large X. The crowd watch with high expectations until the anticipated celebrity does not materialise.

That's our man Turner, said Bing as a middle aged man exit the helicopter.

Turner is dressed in milky white chinos and a brown sheepskin flying jacket, fur collar pulled up around his neck. His bronzed skin, extenuated by wavy silver white hair, radiates good health and understated wealth. Disappointed, the crowd fades away.

Only Bing and Chip stay to greet their guest.

Good to see you Bing and it's even better to meet you Chip, I've always followed your career, envied your achievements, said Turner, shaking Bing's hand and then Chip's. Thought you and I could grab a few holes on the golf course before it gets too dark. Just the two of us. It's on my bucket list.

Playing with a champion golfer, one of fifty things to do before I join my son.

Sorry to hear about him, said Chip instinctively, was it recent?

Seems like yesterday, died for Queen and country, the ultimate sacrifice. One of my jobs, his legacy, is to make sure he did not give up his life for nothing. Love the golf course, very impressive from the skies, said Turner, placing a hand on Chip's shoulder. Did you design it? You've done a sterling job.

Took three years to get it into shape. You play, Chip asked.

You bet I do. Not to your standard. Not in a million years. That shot over the water in the Open. You must wake every morning, kicking yourself. Half a club too short, said Turner.

Thought I'd always get other chances, said Chip, another shot. Never came my way. Always imagined it would, time ran away with me. Chip felt comfortable in the older man's company. Normally he'd not allow someone to invade his space and be so familiar. It also felt strange talking openly about the tragedy on the golf course, not fashioning a joke about one of the single most devastating public humiliations a sportsman should have to endure. The media, but not the golfing public, crucified him for bottling a certain win and never let him forget his capitulation. It was an act of self-destruction for which he would always be remembered. When they wrote his obit he would be the man who threw away the Open and unknown millions. He never let on how much it hurt and how it still gave him nightmares; the same conversation over club selection, an eight or a seven; the uncertainty when he needed a decisive caddy, somebody like himself who can make good decisions with the utmost conviction and confidence.

Most of us never even get close to what you achieved, you

114

and your family should be very proud, said Turner. How did you cope in the aftermath?

Good question. Post traumatic stress disorder for golfers would not be recognised by the medical profession as a genuine ailment. I found relief in the arms of those I loved. My family helped. My wife, before she followed another route. My child. Tremendous support. Without them... But it's all a very long time ago. Life moves on.

Everything starts and ends with the family Chip. May I call you Chip, asked Turner. Hope I am not being over familiar. Kipling never got over the loss of his son in the Great War and I'll never get over the loss of mine fighting another war that is just as important for us to win. Family gives us order. Gives us a reason. Shall we play a couple of holes? I grabbed this all-in-one club on the way out of the house. A good friend lent it to me. An American, who has sadly passed. You adjust the head. See? Turner demonstrated for Chip.

There's no money in clubs like that, said Chip. What's the point of selling one when you can sell 14, plain dumb in my book. Chip was caught between a rock and a hard place. He was pleased to be able to meet Turner yet at the same time he also wanted to watch Eddie cleaning up at Candy's World. He would watch the tape later, slow motion the highlights. Eddie sticking the assassin. Eddie sticking China. Ged could do Eddie, start Monday morning with a clean slate.

Five minutes later Turner pings one down the first fairway, not bad for an amateur. Anything you'd do to improve that shot, he asked.

I'll tell you after I've hit mine. Chip tees up, remembers Bing's advice about selling to potential investors in the resort. Make them feel special. Don't humiliate them or undermine their confidence. Don't thrash them at golf and make them feel inadequate. They won't buy if they feel crap about themselves. Silly Bing with his love struck blustering and crass slogans and mottos. He does not understand the winning mentality. Winners have to win. Second best might as well be last. He rips it, hard as he can. No pressure on the shot other than offloading several tons of angst and a severe migraine. Most of all, he wanted to show Turner he was nobody's pet monkey.

Wow, said Turner, grinning from ear to ear. Worth the flight just to witness that. Let's walk and talk. Forget the buggies. They are for old men. I am glad you didn't hold back to try and impress me. Would have been the wrong thing to do.

Like the mess this afternoon? I had it planned to run like clockwork, said Chip

Bing told me on the phone. A bit of collateral damage, a dead policewoman and a child caught in the crossfire. Shit happens, said Turner. What can we say?

Thanks for recommending your chap, it could have been worse without him. My Merry Men can be a bit wired at the best of times, always have been.

No problem, Jak's a good egg, a family friend, a close friend of my late son, the last human to see him alive. We have a special bond. He's like a second son to me, hate to say it but I've grown very fond of him. Too fond some might say. Causes a lot of jealously with others when you show too much affection to a single person.

You must miss your own son very dearly, said Chip, wondering if Eddie had sliced up Turner's very special friend and his own daughter yet.

Like you and your wife. You've never remarried, said Turner.

No, too painful, said Chip.

Why was the accountant's immediate dispatch so important, asked Turner, changing the subject.

The truth, asked Chip.

That's all I am ever interested in.

He was putting this entire project at risk. Would have cost a lot of people a lot of money, including Bing and me. My life's work, my savings, said Chip.

What did the police have on him, asked Turner.

He was going to do a deal with them, immunity from protection if he grassed us up, me and my Asian friends, who are doing some wholesale import business with substances that the authorities consider dangerous, said Chip.

Commerce should not suffer, said Turner. What did they have on him?

He was a kiddy fiddler, said Chip.

Bastard. I'd castrate them all if it was up to me. If you'd told me I'd have given you a discount on Jak, twenty percent off for deviants and perverts who abuse children. No questions asked. Let's get back to the game. What do you recommend here? An eight iron? Turner had a bit of a dry sense of humour about him.

I should dock you a shot for asking, joked Chip. Did we agree a coaching fee for this?

Turner ignored him and concentrated on his approach to the green. To the right and a dozen or so yards short. We should have agreed a handicap, said Turner. You'll be well inside my ball.

Hopefully. Golf is a hobby for you. It's my livelihood, said Chip.

Amongst other things, said Turner, marching on ahead towards Chip's ball. Don't worry about this afternoon. You were decisive. Took action. Didn't procrastinate and you're fronting up with me pretty impressively. I like those attributes in a man. Seriously. Play your shot first. Then we'll discuss our unfinished business and why I've flown here for our chat. Chip takes the wedge in his hand and swivels it like a drum major's stick, the twirling an early marketing gimmick that became an annoying habit hard to kick. Thinks of the instruction he gave to Amy earlier in the day. Pictured the stance she took. The muscle patterns he outlined. He relaxed. Felt the tension evaporate from tight shoulders and arms. Good enough for her, good enough for him and far too good for Turner. Like a hot knife slicing through butter, a beautifully smooth swing slices under the ball, pitching it twenty feet past the flag. Turner smiled, no doubt thinking it would run through the green. Chip knew better. The ball bites as it hits the turf, the spin kicks in and back it comes towards the hole. An eagle would have been an amusing tale to tell in the bar afterwards. Chip settles for a guaranteed birdie when the ball stops six inches from the hole.

Bravo. Bravo. Any tips on chipping in, said Turner, clearly enjoying the golf lesson. I'll give you this hole and I'll cut to the chase. I'd like to invite you to join me, us, in our, what shall I call it, our syndicate, a kind of Lloyds List for like-minded kindred English spirits. You understand?

Chip was stunned and speechless. Chip thought he was about to be bollocked for the shooting and the attention it would attract with a child and a police officer dead. Turner wasn't bothered in the slightest. He thought he was in for a financial spanking rather than being asked to join an exclusive club. What's the catch, asked Chip.

No catch. Forty per cent of everything you earn goes to the syndicate, said Turner.

Not an invite after all. Blackmail, the bastard was blackmailing him. Bing and his mate had stitched him up. Another time, a less public place and he'd have heaved the wedge through his skull. Instead he smiled, flicked the ball off the surface of the green and caught it one handed. Why would I want to do that, asked Chip.

Because the syndicate protects you, said Turner.

From what?

Everything. As a fully fledged member of the syndicate you pledge 100% loyalty, 100% openness and 40% of your earnings. In return, it's like having a FREE black American Express card. Gets you anything you want in the world, anywhere, as long as you respect the spirit of the syndicate and don't become a Champagne Charlie drawing attention to yourself like a Chief Jerk Officer.

Did Bing nominate, Chip asked, still thinking he was being robbed blind.

Not Bing, he's only an associate. Too soft. Too liberal. Not ruthless enough. His moral compass points in the wrong direction.

And mine doesn't?

None of my business how you do your business. The syndicate is about profit. Generating cash and profits for us all to share. Naturally, we'd push for investment in Paradise Hills, help shift those very nice lodges. We know a lot, and I mean a lot, of very wealthy people with plenty of spare cash for the right investment with the right people. Your story is our story, said Turner. You don't need rag heads. Personally, I'd take a rubber baton to the feet of the Khans, waterboard the bastards just in case they know shit but their money is as good as anybody else's. Your choice. Only stipulation is honesty from you. No lies. That sound OK?

Who else is a member, asked Chip, not believing what he was hearing from Turner. Word of mouth the best sales channel in the world. He didn't understand the financials. That had been Chris DeVeres' domain before he died but he understood what Turner was offering him was priceless. He would be a fool not to accept although he needed to ensure the other business was off his plate as well.

You'll meet them over time.

The assassin?

Jak? No. But that reminds me. He's called me. Told me about the extra fee you'd promised. You owe us additional commission. Keeps the numbers accurate and above board. He'll be well away from you now. Joe is always very punctual. Jak's a good boy, he knows the rules. He gets caught, he takes the rap by himself. Of course, we look after him so the rap isn't really much of a rap. You want to join? We only invite you once.

Forty per cent of lots is better than fifty of fuck all. I'd be delighted and honoured. They shake hands.

Welcome to the club, my 2IC Frank King will be in touch with the paperwork, said Turner, your drive?

One thing, said Chip, unsure what has happened in Candy's World and unable to check on his phone in Turner's company. I may want Jak to go back to the house. Dispatch the girl as an immediate priority. Asking him for the favour assumes no pre-knowledge of Eddie seeking revenge. Chip admired his own nerve and fast reactions.

Why, asked Turner.

She's a witness. Seen too much. She might talk.

Isn't she your daughter?

Was. Not anymore. China's burned her bridges, the Girl Who Cried Wolf. She's too destructive and I am worried about my granddaughter, said Chip, who expected family man Turner to argue the toss but he already had his mobile out.

Joe. Jak. Turner here. You need to turn around and go back to Candy's World.

20: JAK

My name is Joe, I am your driver for the journey south. Should take about three or four hours traffic permitting. On a Sunday we should get a clear run. We'll arrive at the airport with plenty of time for you to catch your flight. Turner has arranged for a young lady called Jan to look after you once I've dropped you off.

Stop the car for a second, said Jak.

Joe does as he's told.

Jak looks back down the road at Candy's World.

He was sure he'd seen Eddie skulking in the bushes. Perhaps his eyes had deceived him.

He knew they hadn't.

He was trained to spot and observe movement, often spending days at a time watching.

Not moving, crapping and peeing into a silver bag, waiting for an opportunity for a single shot or an order to withdraw without contact. A two man op team, like him and Alex

Turner, side by side, ignoring the increasing frustration of his partner, knowing that he is reaching breaking point and ready to snap.

Carry on, said Jak, maybe Eddie was her man, an alternative fat White Stallion Man. He was familiar enough with the layout of Candy's World, had found the booze easily enough.

Not sure about the back of the car's layout, only just taken this job up. About an hour ago. There are DVDs and a variety of drinks. No smoking mind, makes the car stink for days after, impossible to shift the smell. The old boy hates smoking. He says clients always complain about stale cigarette smoke, you know what I mean, said Joe, who sounded like an airline pilot delivering his pre-flight lecture before take off. He's the same with that bloody flying bird. Keeps it bloody spotless himself. Frowns at anyone suggesting drink, food or a sly puff while he's at the controls. Might even see it above us. He's flying up to see your buddy Chip, that crap chubby golfer who bottled it big time. Hit the ball in the water like a big wuss. I'd have made that shot no problem, like I'd have made the shooting today a lot less bloody. How the fuck do you manage to shoot a four year old?

Joe the Lionheart's words of bravado fly straight over Jak's head, who feels bad, really bad about leaving the girl without a goodbye or a thank you for her generous hospitality.

But what could he do?

So Chip was a child abuser.

Had abused the girl with no name when she was six, although it was only her word against the golfer's, an unproven allegation.

Not his fault.

Not his responsibility.

What was worse?

Sexually abusing a child or killing one stone dead in a botched shooting on a wet Sunday morning or shooting one in the head on the side of a mountain in Afghanistan because you were bored shitless and a grinning happy goat herder got on you nerves?

It was a good thing people weren't interested in exploring the cesspit that was his mind, merely exploiting his ability to wipe out life and execute orders without appearing to trouble his conscience or to ask the simple question: *why are we doing this?*

There was nothing he could do for her. Tell social services even though she is now clearly an adult capable of speaking up for herself? Or tell the police? Perhaps he could tell Turner not to do business with Chip anymore? As if anyone cared what he thought or said, especially Turner, if you believed all what Alex said about his old man.

Not his fault.
Not his responsibility.

How long have you worked for Turner, asked Jak, opting for banalities to water down his guilt.

Perhaps he should have helped her.

But that would jeopardise everything he had rebuilt, catapult him back into the bottomless bottle of doom.

All my life, said Joe. You?

We go back a few years. I knew his son first. Then him. He gave me back my self-respect, said Jak.

I am going to miss him when he's gone. Last of a dying breed our mutual friend, said Joe.

What's up with him, asked Jak.

The blood cancer. Leukaemia, direct from the horse's mouth, not that he'd tell anyone outside of his special family. Far too proud and brave. Pretty advanced. Radiation and chemo not working for him.

I am gutted. We had a really special relationship. You sure about the cancer, asked Jak, hoping Joe was misinformed.

Turner would have confided in him unless their own special relationship was a sham.

Perhaps all Turner wanted was the truth about Alex. If he knew, what good would it do anyone. Why destroy just for the sake of it?

Perhaps Joe was right, Turner's impending demise was a private matter, nothing to do with him.

Just like the girl and Chip and the six year old he'd never met.

It wasn't his responsibility.

Like the nameless four year old wasn't his fault.

Not really.

Because if it wasn't him, it would have been somebody else doing the shooting.

Way of the world. Life was like that that song she'd played when they were boning: Wicked Game.

Exactly.

Life was a series of wicked games.

You did the best you could.

Lived as honestly and fairly as you could until leukaemia, the bottle or a Black Talon bullet ended things.

He reached for the brandy.

Unscrewed the top.

Raised the bottle to toast Joe.

Wondered where he would wake up and if he would remember how he got there.

Then Turner called. Joe. Jak. Turner here. You need to turn around and go back to Candy's World.

Once Joe had turned around, Jak confided in the driver that he hadn't expected the call from Turner, thought all the business in the city had been concluded to everyone's satisfaction.

Thing you got to understand about Turner, said Joe, is that he is a very complex character, way beyond your scope and intellect I am afraid. I've studied human nature, got a Masters, and I know his motivations. On the surface he may appear to want one thing but deep down inside he's enjoying the opposite. Do you really think with all his connections he doesn't know how Alex really died? Think about it Jak, said Joe, laughing at him in the rear view mirror. Why is he interested in you? Why does he keep saving you? What pleasure can he derive from seeing you cry your eyes out like a little baby in a hotel room in Dubai, threatening to blow your little brains out. Go on, have a drink son, give Turner the pleasure of seeing you weep and piss your nappies one more time before he pops his clogs.

Jak smiled back at Joe, raised the bottle.

Never knew taxi drivers could be so illuminating.

Cocky and full of bullshit yes, illuminating no.

21: CHINA

Where is he, asked Switchblade Eddie, glancing at her slumped against the wall, before fixing his eyes on the wide open front door and then the stairs.

He must have come in through the rear, used his house key.

He's walked straight through pools of Jack, chilli and bolognese, messy bastard.

Gone, you're safe. My Scary White Stallion Man has ridden off into the sunset.

I wasn't scared, said Eddie.

Sure Eddie. You watched him leave, didn't you? I bet Chip sent you. Wound you up like the spoilt little brat you are.

Watch your lip China, or I'll knock you into next week. Cut you up bad, said Eddie.

Only if Chip lets you, my Big Brave Sugar Puff Honey Monster, mocked China.

She was exhausted and spent. Plan A had failed dismally,

126

Chris DeVeres unexpectedly shot down dead. Plan B had failed dismally. The gunman, the White Stallion Man, had gone. She had started to run and then stopped. Her energy had evaporated. She accepted her fate for disobeying Chip, was ready for the inevitable beating that was coming her way. That's why Eddie was here. To punish her for trying to turn Jak. For disobeying Chip. Telling Jak the bathroom 'suicide' story. Talking about the child abuse when she swore blind that she would never utter another word, although swearing to a monster who entered both her bed and her aged six shouldn't really count.

Do your worst, she said, grateful it wasn't Ged about to dish out the punishment. Sadistic Ged was nasty, enjoyed inflicting pain.

She shook her head slightly in resignation.

It was not meant to be like this. Not meant to have deteriorated out of control so rapidly and indiscriminately. Across the room she catches his eyes, trying to ascertain the malevolence levels after his earlier exertions, aiding the slaughter of innocents. Maybe he would match Ged as Jak had damaged his pathetic macho ego.

A helicopter above momentarily breaks the silence. A celebrity or successful business man visiting Paradise Hills, another fool about to be parted from his money.

As the noise fades, she glances around for weapons. What a shame she had spilled the chilli and the bolognese. The boiling contents might have damaged Eddie or at least given him food for thought before he hurt her. She grins inwardly at the futility of it all.

Was this how her mother felt when she cut her own wrists? Had she known what Chip was doing to her daughter? Chip in Spain playing golf, so they said. She had read the news reports, everything she could about her mother. Searched the internet. Searched her own memories. Her mum kissing her goodnight, calling her a good girl. Then gone, never to be seen again, unsure if it is a real memory or a dream. In other dreams she hears male voices, sees her drunkenly splashing about in the bath. Did Chip drive her to secret drinking? So much she did not and would never know. She smiled ruefully at the futility of it all.

What's so fucking funny? Chip said you and that cunt were taking the piss out of Jimmy, disrespecting me and my family. Even your old man thinks that's unacceptable, said Eddie.

China laughed again, you're a monosyllabic moron Eddie. Shit in bed, shit in the head. Always was and always will be. You and all the other retards cursed with the Doyle name.

I'll cut your tongue and make you eat it bitch, he said.

Sure Eddie, explain that to Chip, said China. The click of the knife startles her.

She hears the sound first, then sees the blade clenched in his right hand.

Fuck.

She is up and running for the front door. He has Chip's permission. Chip's blessing. Eddie's acting on Chip's orders. This is the moment she'd been expecting all her life, since the age of six, when he'd first raped her. She had lost count of the encounters after that. Not just him, his friends, Ged, Chris and Harry. Others too.

China screams to release the adrenalin. Ten strides to the front door, a sidestep.

She outpaces fat Eddie easily if she gets to the door before he bounces her into the wall.

He lunges, she leaps, he skids and misses. The bottoms of his shoes slippery with chilli, bolognese and Jack D. She's outside free, hears a thud and the sound of breaking glass. She's never loved the sounds of breaking glass more. Run China run. Go and get Rose. Room 203. Fight for her. She won't win. But fight for her. Make the effort. She runs ten yards, twenty and stops. He's not following. She looks back. Eddie has fallen through the window and isn't moving. Slowly she inches back to the house, ready to run again should he be trying to con her. Except he's not. Eddie is flat on his back, a thin bloody shard of glass sticking out of his stomach. Above him hangs a double glazed guillotine blade ready to fall and slice him in half.

Shit Eddie. What have you done? I'll call an ambulance, said China.

No. No. China. Hold my hand. I don't want to die alone, his voice weak, a barely audible whisper.

Hang in there Eddie, she said. I'll find something to stop the glass falling.

She looks around for objects to block the gap. Cannot see anything appropriate.

I can't feel anything China. Just hold my hand, pleaded Eddie. Could she trust him? There was an incredible urge to let him die a slow painful death. She couldn't do that with his face full of pain and fear. You could see the soul through the eyes and Eddie's was getting ready to emigrate to the stars.

I am sorry China, so sorry. We had some good times, didn't we? Make sure my funeral is a celebration. Top tunes. Chip might be annoyed at me. Annoyed at the world. Why did he hate you so much China, his own daughter, why did he hate you? He wanted me to kill you. Why would a father do that, asked Eddie, his voice getting weaker with every syllable. China held his cold hand, knowing she didn't have the answers, would never have the answers. Why would a father abuse a child? Climb into the bed beside her and rape her at six. She did not know. Nobody in the world would ever know or understand the minds of men who could do that to children.

Bet Jimmy didn't expect to see me so soon, he said, a weak grin on his face. I cannot feel my legs, or you holding my hand. I am not going to be a cripple.

Let me call you an ambulance, said China.

No, no ambulance. Let's sing a song like we did in the old days, when we were happy, said Eddie.

What would you like, she asked, knowing it was not an appropriate time to define happiness with a man who had failed her on all fronts, a man she'd seduced in the hope he would save her from Chip and Ged and Harry and Christian DeVeres.

You choose, he said, weakly.

China sang about lifelessness on a summer evening, standing there, drunk to hell. She sang, softly, gently, at odds with Shane McGowan's original raucous version with the Pogues.

Beautiful China, I loved that song, me and Jimmy, we'd play it over and over and over, said Eddie. Dirty Old Town too. That was us to a tee. Us Doyles, Irish immigrants in a dirty old town.

They sang together. About an old man. In the corner. Next to the water lilies. China gripping Eddie's hand tightly. Eddie sang by himself, about Johnny singing on the jukebox and love. She let go of his hand so she could call an ambulance on her mobile.

I never found love anywhere China, only in family, little as it was. I enjoyed that though, said Eddie, as the glass fell and chopped him in half. China scampers backwards to avoid the spurting blood, thinking, to his credit, he died silently with dignity, the opposite of how he lived. Goodbye to A Pair of Brown Eyes that never found a purpose.

22: DEEKS

Men in positions of power were stupid, always have been and always will be. Power seduces, foolishly encourages infallibility, a sense that they are above the law, beyond being held to account.

Deeks can see Harry making another call on his mobile in the reflection of the office window.

He's too dumb to know she's watching or perhaps he's too blasé to care.

She doesn't know anymore.

Who is he warning or what's he setting up?

She calls her office to tell them she's not able to identify Cindy at the morgue and delegates Minty and Boucher. Let them share the nightmare of seeing Cindy with half her head missing. Teach them to bitch behind her back, undermine her as a person, a woman and a work colleague. Ironically, she was doing a pretty good job of undermining herself. There had been enough time at the end of the call to tell Minty and the rest of the team what was going on. An opportunity to share what she knew so she did not go into a potentially dangerous situation alone. They would have backed her, been discreet, except ill-planned operations invariably put people at risk. Without intelligence and planning you were pissing in the wind.

She owed them protection having failed Cindy.

Poor Cindy, alone on a cold steel slab, Cindy laughing at her friend pole dancing, wrapping her legs around the pole in a hilarious imitation of China's highly charged performance. That was the girl's name, China. How could you forget a name that was so odd. China, me old China, who lives in Candy's World.

Harry and Deeks walk to the lift in complete silence, descend to the ground floor like two strangers.

She clutches the evidence bag with the imitation black storage device.

He checks his appearance in the reflection of the stainless steel lift, vanity and power walk hand in hand even when he's up to his neck in the thick stinky brown stuff.

She has the car key fob in her hand and opens the central locking as they approach, going to the driver's side.

An unspoken sign that life has changed. Previously, it was accepted he would always drive, unless he'd been drinking and his eyes had turned.

The car's a mess, said Harry, settling into the slashed passenger seat, pushing yellow foam back under the leather covering. We can burn it out and claim on the insurance after we've finished our business. Power corrupts, Harry, with his gloves off, doesn't even blink at the suggestion he's just made. I'll change the bed. I'll cut the grass. I'll defraud our insurance company out of thousands. She was no better.

Faking evidence, lying to her colleagues. At least she would not claim the twenty she'd given the boy Sonny on expenses.

You know Harry I should be at the mortuary, officially identifying Cindy and waiting for her family to console them. Had to send two of the boys to do my job. Where are we going?

See my informant, he said. Share what we've uncovered with our investigations, clear up any misunderstandings.

Am I at risk, she asked.

With me? Don't be daft. I am sharing information with you because we are colleagues and you deserve to know. I was wrong not to acknowledge that immediately and wrong to have barged in on your investigation with DeVeres. Too keen and perhaps me and my team are partly responsible for the tragedy today. His hand touches hers and lingers and she has to fight the urge not to be sick again.

Where are we going, she asked.

Head towards Paradise Hills, he said. Surprise, surprise, thinks Deeks, at least Harry's not fudging. He's edging her towards something approximating the truth.

Your golf club, she asked.

It's near there, yes, he said.

Who are you going to see?

My informant, he said, adding nothing more, despite her leaving the gap for him to fill. They stop at red traffic lights. Both look down at the evidence bag placed between them. She'd been casual leaving it there when she climbed into the car. Not thinking straight in trying circumstances. Nobody can train you for this. There are no police manuals for discovering the man you shared half your life with is a pervert who gets his sexual kicks out of children. If he makes any uncertain moves she'll pepper spray him. Sod the consequences. Might be a fitting conclusion if they crashed and died together in a road traffic accident. At least their sons would be saved from the shame of a paedophile exposed. The lights turn green but neither of them move. A car behind them beeps.

They ignore it for a couple of seconds before she reacts and drives off.

The dynamics have truly changed. Harry would never let someone do that to him without getting out of the car and remonstrating, bullying the perpetrator, throwing around his considerable bulk and his badge that gave him the power to do as he pleased. At first, that behaviour was gallant. In latter years, as they supposedly matured, it was boorish.

Why was Chris so important to you?

You'll find out soon enough, said Harry.

Why not just tell me, said Deeks.

Better direct, he said. More silence as they drive. He breathes heavily, probably has done all their married life, only now is it noticeable and annoying.

Stop here, he said. She does as she's told. Parks the car in a suburban treelined avenue. Posh houses to the right. The golf course to the left and beyond that the coast. She's been brought up in the city and always viewed the avenue with awe. Where are we going, she asked, already knowing the answer.

You, not we, he replied.

We're going in together aren't we?

Why did you think that?

Because you said you're going to help me catch the man who killed Cindy. A fellow police officer, our friend, in case you've forgotten, said Deeks.

When did I say I was going to do that, asked Harry.

In your office. She has assumed... wrongly. It was implicit.

Not to me it wasn't, said Harry. You want to find Cindy's killers go to the white house with the glass dome on top. You can just about see it there. It's called Candy's World. She

134

looked through the trees, spotted where he meant. A glass dome ringed by a balcony. It was a spectacular residence in anyone's terms. Those views of the fairways and the ocean alone would be worth the price of the property.

She goes to open her door.

Hesitation fosters self doubt, gives her time to talk herself out of a tough decision.

Cindy was straight in there and died because of her impetuousness.

Harry reaches across and stops her momentarily, adds to the doubt.

There's an alternative, he said, we can drive on down the avenue and torch the car, forget we were ever here, pretend today never happened. We'll walk to the golf club, have a drink or two and a taxi home. Call the car in stolen in the morning. It's not too far fetched.

It's criminal behaviour Harry, she said.

We're allowed some leeway after what we've sacrificed for the community, the odd perk where the law can look the other way, he said.

She reached down for the evidence bag.

His clammy hand was on hers, preventing her lifting it.

Think about our three boys Sophie, put them first rather than yourself and your pious moral principles. Our three boys don't deserve the ignominy your ludicrous false allegations are going to bring down on their innocent heads. I know I am innocent. I know you're upset because of Cindy and in the cold light of day you'll see the truth but others won't. Mud sticks. The finger pointing, the spectre of the paedophile, that's a horrible word, following them wherever they roam or run to get away from the living hell you've created for them. I won't allow you to ruin their lives as well as messing up mine. You know your allegations could end my career.

The least she could do was give him 60 seconds to think about it out of courtesy for the rare good times they had shared.

Let's continue from your point of view Harry. I am being dramatic, female overkill as usual. Perhaps it's because I am on the rag, my hormones are all out of kilter Harry. Perhaps that's why I am acting like such a daft bitch. After all, what's on this stupid hard drive? A few films and photographs of children having consensual fun. You're observing. That's all. You've never touched any child. Never went near flesh and blood. And it's my fault really. I am frigid, sexually unadventurous, content to lie there with the lights off, thinking about eating peaches, one eye on the clock and the other on my make up to ensure I didn't damage the mask I've worn since the day I met you because clearly I make you very fucking unhappy Mr Harry fucking Wade.

There is a lot of hate inside you Sophie. Make sure it doesn't eat you up, said Harry.

She removes his hand from hers.

Pulls the key fob from the ignition.

He's right.

Of course.

She could do what he suggests.

Walk away from it all and bury it in her subconscious, hope that it would not come back to haunt her when God or whoever controlled everything asked her to account for her life on earth.

She's equally aware she could be walking into a trap set up by Harry and his fellow paedophile cohorts.

Who could blame her?

Let Harry think he's won.

Bide her time and do it all above board rather than be cavalier, charging in where angels fear to tread.

What would Cindy do?

What did Cindy do?

She put others first.

A paedophile like 54 year old Christian DeVeres working in Candy's World pretending to be a 15 year old skateboarder grunge kid and chatting to a 28 year old police constable imitating a vulnerable 13 year old teenager. Chris and his two thousand a month for a six year old called Rose.

What's the house with the glass dome and the balcony called again Harry, she asked, taking the evidence bag with her.

Candy's World.

Funny name. You been there before? You sure you don't want to come with me? Contaminate the place with your fingerprints. A six year old lives there. You know that don't you?

Harry stares ahead, no longer engaging, eyes vacant.

Deeks gets out of the car, barely managing to stand without her legs giving way.

She's scared, terrified.

Come on, says a voice in the back of her head, a voice she'll never hear again.

Some Cindy talking.

OK, Cindy, OK. Either I'll find out why you were shot or I'll be joining you in the clouds. If I am, we'll have one hell of a party in heaven tonight.

23: CHIP

You sure about your daughter Chip, it's a big step to murder your own child, asked Turner.

It's her or me, said Chip, like it was Chris DeVeres or us. I've worked too hard and for too long for it to fail because of a vindictive girl weaving lies and false allegations.

Can't you just section her, lock her away and drug her up to the eyeballs? You know I am not totally comfortable with this, said Turner, standing on the green, putter in one hand, phone in the other.

To be honest, I am not even sure she's mine. Not like me at all. She's unstable, same promiscuous nutty genes as her mother, who killed herself, slashed her wrists in the bath and left her daughter unattended while I was playing golf in Spain. You've heard of the boy who cried wolf, well she's the Girl Who Cries Wolf. Has done all her life. Even tried to copy her mother. Same way, slashing her wrists in the bathroom when she was pregnant. Having sex at twelve or thirteen with any old Tom, Dick or Danny she could find. She was very lucky I found her, said Chip, answering his own mobile and immediately recognising Harry's monotone voice.

She's at Candy's World like you suggested. Make it quick and painless. She's still my wife, the mother of my children. Call me when it's done. I'll wait in the car, said Harry.

Will do. Make sure your alibi's tight, said Chip, thinking what would Eddie do when he encountered an unannounced guest. Presumably he'd dispatched China by now.

Your man has two to exterminate. A lone wolf policewoman called Deeks is close to exposing your buddy. We need to act now before it escalates.

Turner shrugs, makes the call.

Joe. Jak. Turner here. You need to turn around and go back to Candy's World. Two women there. You need to dispose of them both pronto. Same exit plan. No questions needed. Just do as I request. There is a pause. Turner listens. We'll discuss that later. Right now the priority is operation clean up. The sooner the better. Understand Joe? Jak? If you've lost your nerve Joe will do it. It's been a long stressful day.

Turner was spot on the button.

It had been a long day but the end was close.

Rivers of blood would be flowing through Candy's World as the body count rose but fuck it.

Ged never questioned the need to act.

Ged understood.

When he was back and the Khans were sorted, he'd let Mr Grant sort out whoever needed to be sorted, Eddie, the monkey or both.

Like when his wife slashed her wrists in the bath. Ged had seen the problem coming. His wife had confided in him. Silly woman. Told him she was thinking of going to the police. Ged had acted. Gave her an option. Her or China. Forced vodka down her throat until she was unconscious, placed her in the bath, slashed her wrists and watched the blood drain out of her.

Salt of the earth.

Thanks for sorting that out, another hole and then we'll call it a day, suggested Chip after Turner had finished his short call.

We'll make it interesting, two shots, Krug for the winner, you get the half.

You're heartless Chip, said Turner, his concerns forgotten in the name of good business. England needs more men like you.

Chip smiled.

Pictured Amy swinging and relaxed.

24: JAK

He imagines the brandy touching the back of his throat. Before he gets the chance to unscrew the top off the bottle the mobile rings.

Joe puts the call on loud speaker.

A familiar voice, one that sounds imperceptibly weaker following the revelations about the blood cancer.

Joe. Jak. Turner here. You need to turn around and go back to Candy's World. Two women there. You need to dispatch them pronto. Same exit plan. No questions needed. Just do as I request.

Not sure I am happy doing that. Not the girl and her daughter. Besides, we should be more interested in you and your health, said Jak, thinking momentarily why is Turner speaking to Joe first. He's a taxi driver with a highly inflated opinion of himself. Then lets it slide. Another drink and it won't matter who was mentioned first or second.

We'll discuss that later. Right now the priority is operation clean up. The sooner, the better. Understand Joe? Jak? If you've lost your nerve Joe will do it. Turner ends the call as abruptly as it started.

A different Turner from the one who normally spoke to him, cold and detached like Alex had said. Jak swallows, a smidgeon of the raw fluid burns the back of his throat.

He replaces the cap but holds on to the bottle. *If you've lost your nerve Joe will do it. It's been a long, stressful day.* The first put down, the first suggestion he was not capable, a negative comment amongst all the positives.

Or is it?

Another interpretation, Turner was giving him a way out so both men would save face. All he has to do is take another sip and the responsibility is no longer his.

Not his fault.
Not his responsibility.

Joe has permission from above to take over. He expects Joe is the contingency in case he fucks up or implodes. If not Joe, somebody else following him. Turner would never accept complacency or not doing the job properly, unlike his son Alex.

One more sip.
A small action.

You still got the gun? How many rounds left, asked Joe, glancing at Jak in the rear view for affirmation. You take a drink and I'll resolve things. Any intel I need to know?

Only that one of the girls fucks like a rabbit and gives you the best blow job you'll ever have, said Jak, not sure why he's winding up Joe.

I know, I've been watching the two of you at it all day.

Bags it's my turn to ride that bitch bareback up the shitter, said Joe, grinning like a randy goat boy that's been tethered up too long, hope it's not too sloppy after you've had your end away. Jak sees the salacious twinkle in Joe's eyes in the rear view. He's still holding the bottle from the drinks cabinet, wondering why and how Joe would be watching him bone the girl. If he was the insurance policy, why was he stalking him after the successful completion of the operation? Unscrews the top again.

Six not 16.
Not his fault.

He takes a closer look at the face of the man driving the car, searching for genetic similarities and finding them. The genetics and the thoughts and the intentions. The small child herding goats in a far away land was not his fault either. Nothing to do with him.

Not his fault and not his responsibility.

Where was it written that soldiers took the rap for obeying orders when it was the guy at the top of the command chain who should be held to account? He'd used her. She'd tried to use him. That was life. People using each other. Dumping on each other. Then moving on to the next victim. The goat herder was not his responsibility although he'd let them dispense their own justice on Alex. It wasn't his fight, his battle, his war. Never was.

Not his fault.
Not his responsibility.

Joe could handle it all. More than equipped to deliver by

the looks of it.

What are we doing here? A faint whisper. They hadn't communicated for ages. Alex broke the silence. It's too bloody hard. Let's take him out. He's one of them. He's helping them out.

He's a kid Alex, said Jak, a kid herding goats. He doesn't understand anything. Let him be.

I want to fuck him, Jak, want to fuck 'em all. Alex fired and the boy's head exploded.

Shit Alex, what did you do that for? Alex turned and looked at Jak. Did I just do that, he asked Jak.

Yes, said Jak.

One way of fucking him. Oh, well. No need to cover me, said Alex, that was a dumb thing to do. Better go and apologise.

Joe's yapping again.

Breaking his chain of thought.

You know I can take care of all this for you Jak. You just sit back in the car and have a booze. Get off your tits. Black out and run amok in an alcoholic haze for a month or two. Don't worry about getting too far out of it. Turner will come and rescue you soldier boy, if he's still alive. You think he's saving you but you're his toy, his hobby, a Lego toy figure that he can destroy whenever he wants. You think he doesn't know about Alex. Drink up mate. Have a booze on me. No one will mind. I'll sort the bitches out. I'd sort you too for my half brother but Turner's soft on your alcoholic charm. Drink up son. When he's gone, me and you will have a longer chat, Pisspot. Joe hadn't called him a Pisspot and didn't mention the chat or the half brother bit. He didn't need to. His body language and eyes spoke clearly enough of his intentions.

25: DEEKS

Deeks walks slowly from the trashed motor, heels clicking double slow time. She refuses to look back at Harry. Their choices have been made. Two liars. Two frauds. Too bloody much. Her world blown apart in less than half a day. Her precious integrity compromised to the point where she is willingly breaking the law, a law she respected and followed all her life because she thought it mattered more than anything else. How bloody wrong was that? While she walks her slow walk, she hopes Harry comes to his senses, falls in alongside her and they march in unison to Candy's World. Fat chance. She arrives alone at the unlocked front gate, an ornate sign says Welcome to Candy's World. She grasps the pepper spray in her hand, looks up the drive, the light fading fast as dusk falls. The large front door is open. Still time to call for assistance. It's what any sensible person would do, what she's trained to do. Armed response would be with her in a matter of minutes, patrolling the city 24/7, protecting citizens, unseen and unheard. Nothing Harry could do to divert them. What would Cindy do? Could she match Cindy's instinctive bravery and courage. She knew she was behaving irrationally but she could not resist. She wanted to prove to Cindy she had not died in vain. At the same time, test Harry. He would not send her into a life threatening situation, not the mother of their children. OK, he was possibly, probably a paedophile but that did not automatically make him an accessory to murder. Did it? OK girl, left foot first, then the right. One step at a time. She advances slowly, clutching the pepper spray. Halfway up the drive she notices a smashed window and a body underneath. Spray at the ready, she approaches.

A man has been cut clean in half, legs and lower torso in the house, his top half in the garden. She kneels and checks his hand. Warmish. Thinks about closing the lids over his brown eyes. Leaves them as they are, it is a crime scene. There is still time to do things by the book. To carry on is stupidity, an officer of her experience putting herself at risk. Unarmed apart from pepper spray, without any back up or intelligence. Go girl go. She enters the house. There an overwhelming smell of spicy meat. On the table a rucksack and four passports, two UK, two USA. She flicks through them. Two Mackies and two McHales. The same girls. China. Cindy's friend, the queen of the pole dancers at the engagement party. Police. Is there anyone here, shouted Deeks. She hears movement upstairs, rummaging and banging, somebody packing and looking for something, somebody unaware they have company. Slowly Deeks edges towards the central staircase dominating the open plan ground floor and stops. At the top of the marble staircase the pole dancing girl is dressed in a white t-shirt, black jeans and trainers. A different hair style, black hair tied back off her face, free from make up. What's going on China, asked Deeks.

You're Sophie Deeks, Cindy's boss.

Do you know the dead man in the window?

That's Eddie Doyle, said China.

What happened, asked Deeks.

He slipped through a window trying to kill me. I was calling an ambulance and the top half fell on him, said China.

Why was he trying to kill you?

Because I was going to call the police. He's the man who shot them people dead in the city, said China.

Is he? What's he doing here, asked Deeks, motioning for China to come down the stairs towards her.

An ex-boyfriend, said China. Wanted me to hide him and we argued. He tried to shoulder barge me into the wall, missed and fell through the window...you can see what happened to him.

What's going on China? You going away?

Yes, on holiday.

Two different passports?

Dual nationality.

Names?

My mum's.

Your friend in the window? He shot the people earlier today, asked Deeks.

Yes. He confessed. Said he'd shot Chris DeVeres. His brother had slipped under a bus. A policeman and a boy had been hit by mistake, said China.

Policewoman, China. A policewoman, said Deeks.

Man or woman, what does it matter. He did it. Told me so before he died.

Doesn't wash China, said Deeks. I was there at the shooting. Same distance me and you are now from the shooter. Arrogant bastard lifted his visor and stared at me in the aftermath of what he had done. I saw the colour of his eyes. Ice Cold Blue. He's got Brown. Why are you lying, asked Deeks, circling China as she reached the bottom of the stairs. Spray in one hand, cuffs in another. I am going to have to arrest you ….

For what? Telling you the truth. You'll look stupid when you hear my truth. But your kind are not interested in me. My teachers. The police. I told them - you - what was happening. I asked for help but they ignored me.

I am sure we didn't.

Where were you when I was six? You don't know. You're just saying that because you've been conditioned to say it automatically. You plaster on a false look of sudden shock and shame and then you walk away back to your little middle class toffee-nosed tea parties.

This is now a crime scene, said Deeks. We're going to need to secure it. I am arresting you on suspicion of aiding and abetting in the murders of Christian DeVeres, Jimmy Doyle, Wayne Bell and Cindy Taylor.

Cindy?

Yes, Cindy.

My Cindy?

China's legs went, she crumpled to the floor. No, you're messing with my head. I know your game, she said, burying her head in her hands. Deeks moved towards her, unsure whether to comfort or cuff her. The grief and the shock appeared to be genuine.

You were only meant to arrest him and put him in prison so I could get away with my Rose. Put him on remand, cried China.

Who are you talking about? Chris, asked Deeks.

My dad.

Chip?

Yes. It was the only way. Your lot, people like you, never believed me. My word against his so I had to find another way to get rid of him, remove him from my space so I could free myself and my daughter. Not for me you understand. I've had my soul ripped out long ago. But for a tiny little angel, someone who can still be saved because you're going to let me go out the door.

That's not possible and it is not going to happen, said Deeks, you're going to have to come with me. Is your daughter here?

I never meant for anybody to get hurt, cried China.

That's what they all say. Try telling that to Cindy's fiancé, her family, her colleagues, her friends.

I was her friend.

Funny way of showing it, said Deeks.

Not my fault, said China.

That's another thing they always say.

Cindy would want you to help me, said China. She would. If you asked her. Let me go. Give me three steps towards the door and you'll never see me no more.

Is your daughter here?

No, she's probably with her father, said China.

Her father? Who's he?

Her grandfather too, said China.

Stop playing games, said Deeks.

Her father. Her grandfather. He'll be watching us. You're as much at risk now as I am. You wait and see. And on cue, the lights failed and a male stepped out of the shadows, a gun pointing at them both.

Hello girls, Sophie Deeks and China Mackie, I believe.

Hello Jak, said China.

Do you want the good news or the bad news, he asked.

26: CHINA

Hello girls. Sophie Deeks and China Mackie, I believe.

Hello Jak, said China, relieved to see he'd come back despite pointing a gun at her.

Do you want the good news or the bad news, he asked, stepping out of the recesses of the central stairwell that dominated Candy's World. She wasn't sure how he'd got in or managed to cut the electricity, only that he had.

Place the pepper spray on the table behind you. I don't want to have shoot you but I will, he said, addressing Sophie Deeks directly, rather than her, which has to be a good sign. He's on her side. The White Stallion Man minus his horse but still riding to her rescue.

I am not alone. Armed response will be here in a matter of minutes, said Deeks. You might as well drop the gun yourself. Either give yourself up or scarper.

Jak laughs at her. You heard about Black Talon bullets darling? Banned because they do so much damage to the human body. Even the gun crazy Yanks banned the Black Talon. You know why, he asked, about a dozen feet from the two of them, pistol pointed at the chest of Deeks.

You'e surrounded, said Deeks, meeting his ice cold blue eyes without fear. China admires her spunk.

I'll tell you. When this little hollow-point beauty hits your body, it opens on impact, creating six black talons, hence the name. These talons will cut through your organs and shred them. Chances of you surviving are zilch. Now put the spray down now.

Do it, said China to Deeks, please. She knows he has only one bullet left, according to the earlier confrontation with Switchblade Eddie.

Deeks does as she's told. Puts the yellow can down. They'll be here in seconds, she said.

No they won't. We've watched you ever since you arrived. Not been near your phone. And the guy in the car is sitting there pulling on his pecker.

We?

Me and my randy mate Joe. He's outside now. We're cautious. Trained to be wary. And he's the bad news. He'll be coming in when I call him and he's not nice and friendly like me. He wants to party with you both.

Jak?

Yes, China. Nothing, the half formed question evaporated the second he responded, said her name. He'd never used it before. Had he heard all the conversation with Deeks?

Is that Eddie there in the window, asked Jak.

China nods, slowly, watching Jak bend to pick up the switchblade from the floor, lowering himself without taking his aim off the policewoman. How come, he asked.

Chip sent him to stop the rock so I could fall off. Has he sent you to finish what Eddie tried to start?

Might have, he said. Did she believe him? Was he playing

with her? Was the Wicked Game with the world on fire sheer fantasy, her unbalanced mind losing the plot, a mind that conceived a great strategy which backfired when Chip did the opposite of what she thought would happen. Chris arrested as a paedo would grass Chip. They would remand him and she and Rose would run. Contrary to the plan, Chip simply had Chris shot dead in the street by the man expertly retracting the blade into the handle of the switchblade knife. Had him executed in less than 24 hours. Chip had plenty of juice. Chip had tipped himself over the edge, maybe always had been. Maybe her mother... he was away. Ged wasn't. Ged would do it. Was it Ged who had found her? The details were hazy. Snippets from conversations picked up over the years, boys banter while they.... Did they influence her dreams, her truth about her mother. With her gone, all she had suffered would be repeated with Rose. Jak, save Rose for me, said China. Anyone but Chip. Do me if you must but take her tonight. Room 203. Please. I am begging you. Everything I've got. This house.

Shut the fuck up. Sides up close to her. He smacks her hard across the face, stings more than it hurts. Don't move or you'll be dancing your last ever dance with my Black Talon friend, said Jak, reaching for Deeks' handbag and emptying the contents on to the table. He picks up the cuffs, two pairs. How bloody convenient, thinks China. Over by the pole. Circle it. Hold hands. No movement. Deeks does as she is told and China follows, devastated that he hit her. Just like all the others. The smack leaves her speechless. She holds hands with Deeks, feels the cuffs clip on her left, then her right. He's as proficient with them as he is with the gun and the knife.

Joe, shouted Jak. Jak's friend looked like one of Chip's Merry Men, hands virtually scraping the white marble floor, bulky, barrel chested, doubled-chinned.

Jak, our man is still staring at the moon. What do we have here, his voice overflowing with unsatiated lust.

A choice of young and rare meat or something a bit more mature, said Jak.

Men were vile, egging each other to up the ante each time. China blots out the words, concentrates on the woman opposite her.

Just surrender, don't resist. Fighting excites them, prolongs the torture, she whispered to Deeks. She looks into the bluey green eyes of the policewoman, a brave exterior compromised by the fear behind them. She's petrified and with good reason. Just surrender, said China again. Think of something nice, a good memory. It's just your body they are abusing, not your mind. That's yours for keeps. Let them have your body, but not your mind.

Shut up you two, said Jak. Pour yourself a stiff drink Joe. Which one do you want first? China ignored Jak's command to shut up. If it was going to get nasty, she wanted Deeks to know how she felt about the murdered policewoman. I am sorry about Cindy. She was lovely. I never dreamed that this would happen, she said.

Old or young Joe, asked Jak.

Let me have a drink first, rasped Joe, supping Jack straight from the bottle's neck, same as Eddie had done early. They must have copied the habit from a film, thought China, watching him take two or three very large swigs that would render any normal person paralytic. China squeezed Deeks hands, a sign of togetherness in the face of impending sexual assaults, hoping she would understand she could survive what was about to happen to her. She felt Jak's hands, gentle on her hips, moving her 180 degrees to face views of the Paradise Hills golf course. Jak, please save Rose, whatever happens to us, repeated China again.

Who is Rose, asked Joe, is she going to join us?

I'll take the old, you take the new, said Jak, from behind Deeks, one hand holding the gun, running up and down her right hand side, the other stroking her neck. Her eyes closed, surrendering. Jak looks at China, winks at her and sings, *World Was On Fire, Nobody Could Save You, But Me.* He stops his version of the song. Looks towards his mate. Come on Joe, he said. Come and find out what China's feels like. Stop fortifying yourself. She don't bite. Unless you ask her. Mine's a bit tense. But China. She's so bloody horny and up for it. Really lets herself go.

Enough mate, I am in there, said Joe. China feels rough hands between her legs, squeezing too hard. I am not a tit man, Jak. Prefer the meat, said Joe, teeth biting her shoulder. She winces in agony, sees Jak look at her while he plays with Deeks. The pistol pointing to what's going on behind her. A surge of emotion charges through her body. Songs do come true. Words and dreams are real. Jak is her White Stallion Man. She knows, even as Joe strips her bottom half naked. She hears the urgency of Joe's movements behind her, his erection stabbing at her hole. One hand grabbing her hair, the other round her neck.

No Daddy, no Daddy stop, she whispered. She pleads, Daddy, no, not again. Stop them, please. Please Daddy, sobbing uncontrollably.

You're right Jak, she's talks real dirty, really dirty. I am going to enjoy this bag off, said Joe. Keep talking bitch about your Daddy sticking you. Love that big time. She is a wild bitch.

27: DEEKS

Could do with a drink, this one needs livening up, she hears Jak whisper in her ear, feels him take his hands away from her hips. Be back in a moment, baby. Deeks looks at China. Whispering, pleading, begging, for the man with his pants around his ankles to stop. The rapist bashes China around the head twice, hard. Deeks watches Jak through half closed eyes. He walks behind the man called Joe, grabs and lifts the Jack Daniels to his lips before banging it down again. He moves swiftly towards the rapist, his left hand covers Joe's eyes, pulls his head back, exposing his neck, the eight inch switchblade knife plunges deep into the jugular. Blood spurts from the large incision in his neck. Deeks feels warm fluid splash on her face. Another burst showers her top. Jak is twisting the rapist's body and the spouting neck away from her and China. He gently lays the body on the white marble floor and quickly restores China's dignity, gently covering her eyes to protect her from the blood and gore. He says something in her ear Deeks fails to catch, her mind elsewhere as she automatically assimilates what she has just witnessed. She by-passed most of the sexual assault as China had suggested, transporting herself to a fictional graduation ceremony in a grand symphony hall. All three of her boys, investment banker Nigel, advertising executive Colin and student Henry, simultaneously receiving degrees, the warm applause ringing in her ears, Harry, the old untainted Harry, not the perverted queer fish, barely able to disguise his pride at the achievements of his children.

Where are the keys to the cuffs, asked Jak.

Amongst the crap in the bag you've emptied, she replied. Is he dead?

He will be. Sorry you had to see that China, said Jak. You too, I've done a lot worse to people a lot less deserving in the name of Queen & Country.

What happens now, Deeks asked, watching him uncuff them, guiding China to a large leather sofa.

We'll make her some sweet tea, can you put a pan of water on the gas. I cut off the power, apparently they like to film the house from behind the mirrors, he said.

Are they watching now, asked Deeks.

Hopefully not, they outnumber us several to two, three depending on what you do, Jak said, holding China in his arms, waiting for the shock to subside.

What happens now, asked Deeks again, aware the pepper spray and the gun and the knife are unattended. Thinking she has a chance to take control if she can get to them first. Surprise is on her side as he is distracted, comforting the girl.

She walks towards the spray, gun and the knife, watches him watching her, while he strokes China's black hair, her long arms wrapped around him. She pauses beside the gun. She's had weapons training. Could pick it up before he could reach her. She knows it. He knows it. Do you know where the tea bags are, she asked him.

He shrugs, only been here the once, earlier today. Shouldn't be hard for an experienced detective to locate, he said.

She ignores the weapons and the pepper spray, finds cups, tea bags, sugar and a small saucepan to boil the water. Did you have to kill him, she asked.

Either you two or him, said Jak, probably me too. If not today, sometime in the future. Once someone allowed him to exercise his own free will. Silly fool was too complacent, too easily distracted. Once his keks were round his ankles he was dead meat.

What happens now?

You decide. She deserves a free pass. Her daughter too, said Jak.

I've just witnessed you stab a man in the neck, replied Deeks.

Who was about to rape you and her, he said.

You were aiding and abetting. You got a plan, asked Deeks.

I am sure we can come up with one.

How many am I making?

Three. Plenty of sugar. We need all the energy we can get, said Jak.

What are we going to do?

Depends on the intelligence she's able to give us. We do anything blind we're whistling Dixie in the dark, he said. Deeks saw China's hand come alive, squeeze Jak's back, grasp his shirt and cling on to him.

Rose is in room 203 at the Paradise Hills hotel, said China, we have to get her back safe, even if it's the last thing we do.

I know, said Jak.

And thank you, said China. Thank you so much.

28: JAK

The tea is perfect, just the right strength.

Sweet, hot and invigorating.

No other drink boosts moral better than a traditional English cuppa.

Here, have a sip or two, said Jak to China, holding the cup to her mouth with one hand, the other cradling her head.

She does as she is told, takes a couple of noisy slurps. That feel better, he asked.

Yes, China replied, embarrassment and humiliation written in capital letters across her blotchy red face, bruised where the rapist had thumped her. I need to get changed again. I feel filthy. Do you mind? Do you want a clean top, China asked the policewoman.

Deeks nodded, drank her own tea, legs crossed, as if she was at the imaginery suburban afternoon tea party that China had mentioned earlier.

I'll only be a minute or two Jak. You going to wait this

time? You'd better come with me. Your face is a picture, said China to Deeks. You look like an extra from a horror movie. I guess we all do.

Jak watches them go upstairs, traumatised by the last 10 minutes. Seeing a man have his throat slashed has that effect.

He walks over to Joe, his trollies around his ankles, his penis small, limp and pathetic.

He feels in the pockets for ID. A credit card. Joe Reid, the bastard love child of Turner, half brother of Alex.

Probably, possibly not.

It didn't matter.

He'd declared war on Turner and all that he stood for and kissed his life as Jak Hart goodbye.

Everything thrown away but he had finally made a choice.

Up until now, he'd never made a decision, not a real one. Not one that mattered. Men like him were not meant to deviate or change sides. Not with the life they inherited and the way it was designed to pan out. Work, play, rest and die. Quickly and quietly without making any difference to anyone or anything. Reading and writing and adding embarrassed men like him so they channelled their energies into exercise. Nobody cared enough to offer alternatives. If they tried, the crash street kids were too dumb, too jaded, too alienated to notice. Organised sports were their passions. They loved the rules because they gave everything meaning. If you played a game and broke the rules, you were only cheating yourself, even when it was easy to bypass them. They were cannon fodder for the services or the factories or the mines or the dole queues, however the Turners of this world wanted to exploit them. His story was the same as thousands of others, the doomed Soldier in the Harvey Andrews' song, sacrificing himself to those who called him murderer not friend. The government banned it because they were scared it would deter young rebels without a pause from joining up, as if they ever had a choice.

What to do next?
He'd lied to her.

His first kill wasn't at the age of 17, although it was around that ballpark.

He'd signed up for Queen and Country because he couldn't think of anything else to do with himself, the Solider song an inspiration and a catalyst for action, rather than a damp squib.

Found himself fighting in faraway deserts he could not locate on a map for reasons he could not understand, trained to perfection and better equipped than the arab sand soldiers they chased, harried and executed.

After 'liberating' the middle east, the next step was battling young goat herders in the most mountainous terrain he'd ever seen in his life.

Alex Turner shooting the child because he was bored.

Jak had made a choice then or had he?

Don't cover me, said Alex.
And he hadn't.

He had let down Alex and now he was about to do the same to his father, Turner.

He owed him more than he had owed anybody in his life.

The only person who had ever invested time with him, shared what he had without asking for immediate favours in return.

Taking out the two women as Turner ordered would have been over and done in two or three minutes.

Only Joe's raping them would have delayed matters.

He'd have been back in the car and heading south towards the airport and the hideaway by a beach that he'd bought for peanuts when he first started killing people for hard cash.

Nobody would have thought any more or less of him because nobody cared.

Why had he betrayed Turner's trust for a girl young enough to be his daughter, who was probably spinning him a yarn?

Easy.

Real men didn't fuck six year olds.

Real men didn't kill innocent people either.

Turner said there were always good reasons to justify the ultimate action: *We're fighting different wars now, wars without frontiers and boundaries, where the enemy are protected by lawyers and corporations interested only in the bottom line. They have no liability, he said, so we make them liable for their actions. They say up yours to us, we say up yours back with a bit more oomph. We have to protect our way of life, the way we've always lived way back into the middle ages. Without it, we're the same as the sand boys.*

Jak should have asked Turner how the girl was a danger to the country.

He had heard them talking before he'd entered the room, the two women, China blaming Eddie for his actions, protecting him, Jak Hart, professional loner, professional nobody.

He'd deserted her, let her down, yet she had tried to pass the blame elsewhere.

There was no way she knew he was listening.

He'd made the right choice.

The only choice.

Fathers don't fuck six year old daughters.

Or order the assassination of their own children unless they were hiding deep dark secrets.

Or watch them fuck strangers or watch granddaughters they'd fathered play on hidden cameras.

How sick was that?

How evil?

But that wasn't the real evil.

No.

The real evil was knowing what was happening and choosing to do nothing.

Evil only existed and thrived when men and women looked the other way and ignored the suffering of others.

Alex walked from their observation post, not a care in the world as he descended towards the dead boy and his own premeditated death. Jak never questioned why. Never asked himself key questions. Until now. Why was Turner insistent on the truth about the death of his son yet in no rush to discover it? The official report was there for all to see and question themselves. Bits that did not tally could be examined, put under the microscope. Did he already know? Possibly. Perhaps he knew his son too well, knew himself and the genes they shared. Or was it sons. Joe the rapist with the hole in throat. Like father, like son. Jak had been passive with Alex, the line of least resistance. If challenged, he could in all honesty say that he could not have prevented Alex from doing what he did. The fatal shooting of the boy took place without any warning. Alex standing up and walking towards the corpse. Don't cover me. Jak hadn't tried to stop him. Hadn't tried to bring him to his senses. Hadn't called for assistance. Jak watched them come at Alex, still armed with an assault weapon that hung loosely at his side as his attackers lunged. Three of them armed with machetes, hacking at Alex. One second standing there, motionless. The next falling to his knees. His attackers struggling to retrieve their machetes from Alex's bones. Jak had stood up finally

*and exposed his position. He shouted Stop, Enough in Arabic.
Thought it useful to learn the lingo in case you ever needed
to converse with the indigenous population. Might save your
life one day. They'd stopped. Backed off. They knew and he
knew. He could have fired, shot them dead and didn't. He
aimed his weapon and had them in his sights. They weren't
terrorists. They weren't insurgents. Or religious lunatics
wanting to take the world back to the middle ages. Funny
how both the insurgents and Turner's crowd wanted the
same thing. This obsession with the Middle Ages, whenever
that was. People minding their own business, trying to get by
as best they could. Go, he shouted at them, again in Arabic.
Go. He didn't know Arabic for Sorry. Afterwards Jak said
enemy insurgents had shot the small boy. Instinctively, Alex
had broken cover, gone to help and administer first aid, an
instant posthumous hero. Jak had fought them off, got a
medal. What he didn't say was that Alex was still alive when
he got to him and whispered his last words to Jak, words
that Turner might not want to hear, words that Jak had
ignored until now because he'd never had any real context
for them.*

The two women rejoin Jak. They are roughly the same
height, China thinner than the older woman. Faces
scrubbed, damp hair pulled back off their faces.

What do we do now, asked Deeks and China in unison.

Good question, said Jak, the plan worked out when he
knew where Turner was and how he'd arrived at the resort.
You two get Rose. I'll sort out Chip and Turner.

Who's Turner, asked Deeks.

Nobody important. A sick man with cancer and a grudge.
Let's share what we know.

29: DEEKS

Another time and another place Deeks thought Jak would have made a good police officer.

He had a natural talent for collating information from different sources, developing plans and making decisions.

China had sketched a layout of the Paradise Hills resort, marked room 203 where Jenny and Karl Grant were babysitting Rose, the 19th hole bar and the golf shop and Chip's office.

Where would a helicopter land and take off, asked Jak.

China pointed to beyond the putting green.

How do you know all this is accurate, asked Deeks.

Chris DeVeres showed me, replied China.

Were you friends?

No. You cannot be friends with someone who repeatedly rapes you, no matter how polite they are, said China.

Sorry, said Deeks.

Don't, he was Chip's key into the Paradise Hills

development, said China.

Did Chris think that Rose was his daughter, asked Deeks, unable to stop the instinctive detective inside her, recalling Chris's standing order to China.

He might have thought that, yes, replied China, clearly anticipating Deeks line of questioning.

Enough of the small talk, said Jak, studying the resort outline. This is what we are going to do.

He explained their roles quickly, succinctly and authoritatively.

It was a simple plan, not many moving parts to go wrong and relied on speed.

All Deeks had to do was get Rose out of 203 and drive the car around to the far side of the resort where the golf course snaked out onto the coastline.

Is that it, asked Deeks.

That's about the size of it, he said, and forget you're a police officer for a couple of hours. Give her a chance to get away. If our decoy strategy works, she'll meet you at the far side of the golf course. She gets in the car and she's away with Rose. Then you're free to resume the day job and come after me.

One problem, said China. I can't drive.

30: CHINA

The two of them drive into Paradise Hills' sprawling car park in the half dark, pick a spot away from the lights.

Park up and turn off the engine.

Nervous, asked Deeks.

You bet, replied China, so much can go wrong.

Like what?

Being spotted for starters, said China.

She could see the twins Ged and Denzil Grant emptying the contents of a hire truck into Chip's golf shop watched by two large oversized Asians. Ged an enormous build, like one of them heavyweight Sumo wrestlers, and Denzil, the polar opposite, skinny as a rake. Ged the ultimate psychopathic hedonist, the polar opposite to Denzil, who was content to exist almost unnoticed in his huge brother's dark moody, violent alcoholic shadow. Chip was nowhere to be seen fortunately. If he had, it might have rendered China unable to function.

Everything will be fine. Knocking on people's doors is a busman's holiday, said Deeks. It will be a breeze. Nobody will recognise you, not in this light. Come on, let's go.

Give me a couple of seconds to compose myself, said China, running through the plan Jak had devised for her one more time.

Go collect Rose.

Hand her to the policewoman.

Then run through the resort, making sure at least two or three people see you running towards the golf course. Then run as if your life depended upon it.

When you get to the car drive down south to an airport and fly to Paris, France, anywhere out of the UK.

Here's an address for a beach hut, he'd said out of earshot of Deeks.

Said once she went, nobody should EVER know where if she wanted to stay safe.

Not even Deeks.

He'd wished her luck. Kissed her on both cheeks.

What's going to happen to you, she asked him, what can you do with one single bullet and a knife.

My job is to stop the pack chasing you, simple really, he told her.

How you going to do that, she asked.

He'd smiled, Ice Cold Blue Eyes that Melted Her Soul. You look after Rose for me, he said, that will be enough, occasionally play our song, that Wicked Game song that you love playing so much.

You are going to make it aren't you, she'd asked.

Of course I am, I may be dumb and stupid but not that dumb and stupid to... the sentence left hanging. She'd stopped him. Her turn to place her fingers on his lips. Didn't want to hear the word: *sacrifice*. The World Was About to

Catch Fire and the only person who could save her was a White Stallion Man. He was willing to give up his life for her and a little six year old he had never even met. A girl who knew nothing about anything except koala bears were cute and the rock that spins through space was one giant playground dedicated to her happiness.

One thing, I take Rose. Not you, said China, daring the police officer to contradict her, knowing she wouldn't. A mother understands. All mothers do, including her own teetotal mum, not a secret drinker. China would have remembered the smell on her breath. It all made perfect sense. Chip away in Spain. Had to be Ged, bloody Ged.

Deeks knocked on the door of room 203.

Jenny answered it.

Detective Inspector Sophie Deeks. Drugs squad. We've reason to suspect you're in possession of Class A drugs. Go back into the room.

Deeks entered.

Karl Grant was fast asleep on the bed, mouth wide open, snoring. No, don't wake him. You just stand there nice and easy. Who is the girl, asked Deeks.

Rose, I am minding her for her mum, said Jenny.

And who is her mum, asked Deeks.

Me, said China, entering the room on cue. Rose saw her and jumped up into her arms. This is nothing to do with me or my daughter is it?

No, you can go, said Deeks.

Outside China took Rose's hand.

We're going to go play and run about. How does that sound?

Fun, Mummy, fun.

168

31: CHIP

Chip had pulled it off, against all the odds.

The greatest escape beyond even his expectations. He'd gambled, taken huge risks and won.

Ged and Denzil were unloading the drugs.

The Khans were happy and ready to take delivery of the merchandise.

With his share, he'd have control of damn near 50% of Paradise Hills.

One more point and it would be his as the majority shareholder.

Turner's sales would tip the balance his way.

He was moving upmarket, buying into a power structure that had existed since William the Conqueror and them fucking Normans and beyond that even.

All the obstacles that had been placed in front of him had been cleared.

Chris was a weak point and had been executed.

The assassin tying Chip to the killing would be gone too.

So was Jimmy Doyle.

Eddie would follow when Ged cleaned up.

He'd finally called time on China.

Sad but inevitable.

When Rose matured to a suitable ripeness China's days were always numbered.

He excuses himself from the party in the 19th hole. Said he needs ten minutes alone.

Shakes hands with the journalist Anna Judd and the PR Sally Bailey.

They'd lost interest after the jaw breaking anecdote, silly cockteasing whores.

In the toilet he tries to get a live feed to Candy's World. He wants to see the mess Eddie had made of China and Harry's wife and Turner's chum. He'd wait until the police discover the bodies before becoming Rose's official guardian. For some reason, the live feed is down, the screen void. Never mind. Denzil would sort it out. Instead, he views video footage of Amy hitting golf balls, pictures her naked, rather than dressed, himself naked rather than dressed, a crowd watching adds to the thrill. He pulls hard and slow on his penis to prolong the moment of release.

Chip, Chip.

A strong insistent bang on the door. Bloody dopey Karl Grant. China's taken Rose. The police busted us. And there's a bloke covered in blood talking about going up in a helicopter. Wants you to come now.

32: JAK

His plan was bloody risky. Fraught with what Turner
called risky banana skins. Way he viewed it, the plan had
Slim and No Chance. A frizzy haired boxing promoter had
used the quote numerous times on television: *Ladies and
gentlemen, the challenger has No Chance and Slim. And
Slim has just left town.* Not that he'd communicate his
misgivings to the women. They had to believe in the plan
otherwise it would stall and he couldn't allow that.

*His plan. His responsibility. His fault if it went tits up.
Like ignoring Alex cracking up beside him. He knew he was
cracking up under the pressure yet told nobody. His fault.
His responsibility.*

Way he saw it, the plan only worked at high speed, fool
Slim into stepping back inside. If anybody had time to think
it was Goodnight Irene.

High speed. No delays. Or pauses.

Get me Chip. Get me Turner, said Jak to a couple of

restaurant staff sneaking a fag outside the 19th hole. Jak stinks, daubed with the bloody insides of Eddie.

What's up, said Turner, the first out, no time to plaster his usual veneer of detached calm across his inscrutable stoic Middle England features.

The bitch stabbed me with a blade, said Jak, screwing up his face in faked pain, hoping the urgency mitigated his bad acting.

How? Did she escape, demanded Turner.

Slashed me, said Jak, no time for an inquest, we got to find the bitch fast. Get your helicopter up. Our best way of finding her. She has to run by the coast. Joe's got the road covered.

Why won't he answer his mobile, demanded Turner again, speed dialling Joe several times in panic.

Busy checking for China, replied Jak. He's a smart operator. He won't let us down.

Did the policewoman get sorted, asked Turner, looking beyond Jak, trying to spot the girl running in the dark. Turner not thinking, responding to the crisis with wild aggression.

I think so. Joe was looking after her. Mine slashed me and ran away. Feisty bitch. She'll be hiding amongst the trees and the bunkers. In the dark on foot we've no chance of finding her, unless we accidentally trip over her. Best get up high, spot her with the lights. I'll jump out and slot her. Be like the old days with Alex, won't it, said Jak, reeling off the words faster than he's ever spoken in his life.

You're right. Let's get airborne, said Turner. Don't want to waste a minute. As he turned he looked at Jak over his shoulder, a quizzical expression appears on his tanned face. He knows. The bastard knows. Jak's heart misses a beat or two. Turner's sussed him and is about to push Slim further out onto the streets. Instead, Turner grins a crooked smile and shakes his head ever so slightly, as if in admiration for a clever trick he's been shown by a magician.

Seconds later the size of the search party is doubled by number and quadrupled by weight. Chip arrives panting, heavily out of breath, accompanied by a huge overgrown giant of a man with a huge overgrown red beard. This is Ged Grant, my right hand fist, said Chip. He'll help us hunt her down. What's the crack?

Turner explained, briefly, quickly, not hesitating. We're going up soon as she's ready.

Is he coming, asked Jak, nodding towards the red bearded giant, thinking two was company, three was definitely a crowd that he hadn't anticipated having to handle. The big man would take some shifting and unbalanced the odds against him. He'd have to deal with him early doors. Two in the front, Turner flying, Chip can play co-pilot. Me and Red in the back. Doors open all the time so we can spot, jump and grab her. No one will see us, speed-jived Jak. They are rushing. Not thinking. Not considering the situation fully. Caught up in the thrill of the chase. He can pull this off, with a bit of Lady Luck.

Can't we just go out on foot, said Ged Grant. The giant speaks. States the bloody obvious. His opinion is not wanted. Appeal to his macho nature. You worried about the jump Big Man? Piece of cake, said Jak. I've been jumping out of these babies half my life, former red beret, air trooper.

It's our best option. You'd need two hundred plus of us to cover this ground in the same time we can, said Turner, we'll ride low, lights on, zig zag across the golf course and turn over the ocean so we don't miss an inch. Leave the doors open. Hook yourselves in with the safety belts. They'll more than hold your weight, big as you are. You spot her, I'll lower down to twenty feet and then, and then, and then Jak and you jump. Turner had whipped himself into a frenzy in a matter of minutes, the adrenalin junky on a big high he'd never got in the board room or networking with business turkeys. Jak imagined Turner thinking he was General George Custer leading the glorious Seventh into the Little Big Horn, hopefully with the underdogs coming out on top again. Charge. Jak yaks. Whinges about his wounds. The bitch. The bitches. Up in the air. Let the fun begin. Talks so much they cannot think. Drown them in words. Red Ged sits next to Jak in the rear, avoiding touching his bloody body. If they'd had time to ask. Time to think. Jak has misgivings as they climb and he plugs in the headphones. This was such a stupid plan. An unrehearsed jump from an aircraft with rotor blades that will mince you in seconds. If the blades didn't chop you up, the chopper would crush you as it followed you to the ground. Crashing into the water was his only chance of survival although that outcome posed its own unique problems. He would tackle that challenge if he got that far. First Ged had to be erased to rebalance the odds. Bank her to the left Turner, yelled Jak, I think I can see her.

Where, where, yelled Turner, totally caught up in the blood lust, banking the helicopter as requested, dipping more than he should to see for himself. Ged scanning the ground and leaning out, his weight unbalancing the craft further. He was a heavy motherfucker.

A bit more, said Jak, over there. By them trees and the sandpits. They are sandpits Chip. You look shit mate, you're not worried about our pilot and this fragile baby. Big brave man like you? Chip said nothing, face red as beetroot, body hunched up in the small cockpit.

Wilco, said Turner, barely able to contain his excitement.

We're tumbling, shouted Jak, we need to offload. He cut through the strap holding Ged and pushed him out of the

174

gap, stabbing him a few times in the hands and the legs and the buttocks for good measure. Ged tried to stop himself falling two hundred feet into a four hundred year old oak tree and failed. His body impaled on branches that snapped as he crash landed.

How did that happen, did the strap snap, shouted Turner, concentrating on controlling the aircraft after the rapid offload.

Think he fancied a spot of sky diving, silly time for taking up a new hobby don't you think Chip? Bit more dangerous than fucking tiny kids. Jak rammed and twisted the switchblade knife deep into the back of Chip's neck. The point of the blade entered between the two top most vertebra, the axis and the atlas, severing his spinal cord. By the way, did you want me to kill both your daughters, asked Jak, adjusting his position in the craft so Slim could settle into the spare seat recently vacated by Dead Red Ged.

Jak, you've lost the plot, said Turner, realising what had happened. What you fucking done, you gone nuts?

Shouldn't fuck six year olds, should they. You listening Chip? Your two girls are free as birds now, think on that while you drown in your blood. Take us over the ocean, Turner and I'll tell you what Alex told me, said Jak.

What's going on, asked a stunned Turner, clearly shocked. His debonair facade cracked wide open. I understand Post Traumatic Stress Disorder. The four year old you killed today has brought it all back, I understand. You're blaming those two. Let's get down on the ground. Nothing rash. Talk it over man to man.

Just take us out over the ocean my old friend, said Jak, your time is up. If not today, soon and I think you'd like it better this way rather than the blood cancer.

What you talking about, asked Turner, doing as he was told and taking the craft out to the sea. Soon?

Joe told me about your blood cancer before he ended up with a knife in his neck like dickhead here, said Jak, pushing Chip's head forward, aware he was covered in fresh blood.

There's nothing wrong with me. I am in bloody remission, shouted Turner.

Did you know about Alex wanting to leave the army?

Don't be stupid, he loved the life. And he was going to love working for me too.

Alex told me he'd begged you to let him leave the army but you'd refused, said you'd disinherit and disown him. He hated you, said Jak.

Don't be daft Jak, we can talk about this later, I am doing as you say, taking her out over the ocean. You're lying about Alex. He was a good son. He loved me. The syndicate was his when he retired from the services but he needed a commission to match me. He knew that, commission first, then out, said Turner, hovering the craft over the water below, 100 feet above sea level.

I think your bastard son Joe believed it was his syndicate, that was his inheritance. Never told me about him either. Joe reckons you knew about Alex and me and you had an ulterior motive to keeping me by your side, said Jak. Was he talking shit or are you some sort of sick sadist?

You're not a thinker Jak, I loved all my sons, said Turner, let's land and have a chat. You are part of the syndicate too. My riches are all yours. As much as you want. I'll even say Chip and the Red Beard were accidents. I'll protect you. Swear to God.

What's the point Turner. It's over. Like it was for Alex. You want Alex's last words, why he shot the goat herder?

No, said Turner. I don't. Let's talk this over. It's not meant to end like this for me. I don't deserve this. I am a good husband. I love my Veronica. She's got a film premiere tomorrow. She needs me by her side. You too. I am a good father. My girls, they need me. Lost without me, said Turner, sobbing. You're a second son to both of us.

Too late my old friend. You listening Chip, this is Jak Hart's advice for fathers who claim to love their children. The parent and the friends of a young goat herder hacked Alex to pieces with machetes. I stood by and watched him. Not because of what he'd done, because it was what he wanted me to do for him. He didn't want me to save him. *Don't cover me.* He wanted to be hacked to death. His lasts words? *Jak, I shot the boy because he was happy and I was aroused, I wanted to fuck him like my father had fucked me. I never wanted to be that bastard, sorry. I'd rather be dead.* Jak never really understood what he meant until now. Thought he'd meant a mind fuck, not a real one. You always understood that didn't you Turner? Always checking in case he'd told me you'd fucked your own son. In case I remembered.

That's bollocks, I don't believe a word, said Turner. I'll take her back to the resort. We'll have a chat. Have my lawyers give you a large share, all official in writing. You'll never have to work again.

Sorry mate, said Jak, the cancer might not kill you Turner, but I want to be safe from your influence and your money. China and Rose too. And the policewoman you ordered me to kill. Big risks to the state, I think not.

Jak, don't. Please, cried Turner.

Jak moved towards the exit where Ged had fallen and fired the Black Talon round at point blank range down into Turner's head, the bullet exiting and hitting the dash. Goodbye my paedo friends, said Jak, deciding there was no point hanging around any longer than necessary. He tumbled backwards and outwards.

33: DEEKS

Deeks watches the helicopter take off before checking for movement in Harry's car.

Illuminated under an orange street light, her husband sat motionless in the passenger seat.

Maybe he's waiting for instructions from his paedophile friends or definitive conformation that she's gone.

Knowing Harry, he was probably shedding crocodile tears for a wife he despises in the sunshade mirror, rehearsing his grief to play the bereaved husband for all he's worth. Stopping off before the rendezvous point wasn't part of Jak's plan but she doesn't really take orders from hired killers, however exceptional the circumstances.

She'd have sworn blind that Sophie Deeks would never compromise her professional integrity by doing what she'd done today. Her badge and rank less important than her grief for Cindy, her anger at Harry and her compassion for China, the innocent victim. On a wet Sunday in a northern city she could put the victim first for once because she could believe her story one hundred and one per cent. If she was a fraud, why wasn't her father helping her resolve her problems?

Simple question, simple answer.

Because he was guilty.

A good father would have helped his daughter, no matter what the allegation.

A good father would forgive his daughter anything, not order somebody to kill her.

A good father puts his children at the top of the list, not the bottom.

China was no angel, nagging questions would remain, probably unanswered. Was she BudgieBoy? Had she played them? Was she that smart? That manipulative? Now was not the time for pondering the finer detail. A good father would not execute his daughter or allow her to be raped by a savage beast. That overrode every other consideration. Deeks knew she was doing the right thing for China and for Rose and that her God would approve. She was saving them from the trauma of the court case too.

It's the least she could do.

China didn't need to relive her nightmares in a Middle England court, unlike vulnerable Frances Andrade, 48, a violinist who killed herself days after testifying against a paedophile music teacher. Everybody had let her down. Kate Blackwell, QC, the defence barrister in the court who cross examined her without mercy. Judge Martin Rudland, who said Kate's behaviour was perfectly acceptable in his summing up. And the unnamed mental health service professionals, who saw nothing of concern in SEVEN suicide attempts before poor Frances went to trial and met Kate.

Deeks knew there was hundreds and thousands of Frances Andrades in every city, town, village and parish.

Different ages, different names, different narratives but always the same outcome: victims suffering because society was indifferent to their abuse.

Deeks was not exempt from criticism.

She chased perpetrators, irrespective of the price the victim would pay in court and in the aftermath of a guilty or innocent verdict.

Rapists and sex offenders and paedophiles thrived because ordinary people in society thought it was acceptable behaviour.

A man continuing to conduct an orchestra in a cold rainy northern city after serving time for sexually assaulting young boys.

A publicist trading in lies who lived one big lie in a warmer, but emotionally colder southern city.

An accountant in Steel City.

A weather forecaster in Rainy City.

Always somebody in a city or a town or a village or a parish or a street or a house near you, next to you.

The unknown women with the unknown fathers and the unknown nightmares chasing them for eternity, leaping from the shadows when they least expected it.

Bastards all of them.

Fathers who fucked their children.

They would face a dual judgement, one on earth and another in front of God.

They could cheat and deceive the first process but not the latter.

The almighty would see through their lies and punish them. Jak too would have to meet his maker.

Would China's freedom atone for his other sins.

Not for her to say although she'd look the other way on this one occasion.

Harry was not going to get that luxury, not if Deeks had

anything to do with it. She knocks on the car window.

Harry, slightly startled, winds down the window.

She passes the old cassette recorder through the gap.

Smiles her most beautiful, most poignant smile.

Surprise, surprise Harry Wade. Bet you never expected to see your wife again did you Harry. Enjoy your freedom while it lasts because segregated prison time is calling out your name so loud it's giving me a bloody headache. That's solitary to you and me, Harry, because those murderers, rapists, terrorists, gangsters and sociopaths will really hate you because you're police and probably put a fair few of their number behind bars and because you're a bit of a kiddy fiddler and they hate cunts like you who fuck with children. You'll be eating their excrement, drinking their piss and waiting for their knives to castrate you. Don't worry, I'll tell our boys what a wonderful man you were and how lucky they were born male.

She stopped for breath.

Could hear Cindy clapping with delight at her performance.

See her beaming smile rather than the hole in her head. Go Deeks go.

This one is for you Cindy, said Deeks, backing out of the car and discharging half a can of pepper spray straight into his face.

It's not much of a consolation Cindy but it's the best I can do right now.

34: CHINA

Mummy that big flying bird has fallen from the sky into the water, said Rose, pointing to where the helicopter had been before it crashed into the sea.

It's not real, said China to Rose, hugging her close as they jogged in the semi-dark. It's just a toy helicopter. It's really not real. A radio control model. Somebody is flying it from the beach and made a mistake. He'll build another soon enough. We're doing really well, cling tightly to me and don't let go.

Where are we going Mummy, I don't like this, said Rose.

We're going on a great big adventure, said China.

She had to watch the helicopter go down to prove to herself it was over.

Jak hadn't said but she'd guessed.

Once she saw it rise she realised he would bring it down to earth with a huge bang.

It was the sort of Selfless Act a Man Mounted on a White

Stallion would do for a Maiden in Distress and it Broke her Heart.

Why can't we just go home to Rosie's World Mummy, asked Rose, filling up as she clings to China, like a koala to the eucalyptus tree.

We're going on holiday, said China to reassure the child, knowing Jak has taken out Chip and Turner so she won't spend the rest of her life looking over her shoulder. Somebody would do all that for her. Willingly.

He knew her anxiety would be too much, drive her into depression.

Without her support Rose would wilt and fade away too.

Like her, he knew all children deserved unconditional love, without compromise, happiness the only goal.

All that she had missed out, she would freely give to Rose, safe from evil.

Jak's gift to give, a gift he had just freely given.

I don't want to go, whined a very tired Rose.

Why not, asked China.

I like Rosie's World.

Me too, honey, but we're going to go and find a new Rosie's World by the seaside. We'll have new friends... dogs... you'll like that ... you always say you want pets. We can have them at our new place.

Where is it...?

By a beach somewhere..

Where...?

I don't know...

How many dogs?

As many as you want?

I want four. Four hounds. Why are you crying mummy?

Because I am happy, happy and sad.

China and Rose arrived at the rendezvous.

Deeks was leaning on the car bonnet, exuding calmness.

Two minutes to get your breath back and then we're off, she said.

You going to help us still. Now he's not here, asked China.

Cindy would give me a right telling if I didn't deliver what I promised, said Deeks.

Did anyone jump out of the helicopter before it crashed, asked China. I was too busy running to see clearly.

Not that I saw, said Deeks.

Shall we wait and see, asked China.

Not now, let's get you away from this mess.

China climbed into the car and hugged Rose tight.

She would have to let go eventually but not right now.

She wanted to hold Rose tight and imagined Jak's arms around them both.

Save him, if you're up there watching over us my interventionist God.

Save him.

Keep him on the rock.

For me.

Save him from my wicked games.

35: THE BEACH

There is a small restaurant, a stone's throw from a small sandy beach, well off the beaten track.

Hidden away from the usual tourist haunts.

You have to know the area really well or have a quiet word with a friendly local, who may, if they like you enough, share the location with you.

If you are fortunate to ever visit, you will discover an unspoiled corner, a natural paradise, untainted by commerce and the manic desire to make quick tax-free bucks.

The tiny restaurant only caters for two dozen maximum but easily survives on a lot less patronage thanks to overheads wisely kept to an absolute minimum. Fishermen from nearby coastal villages and farmers who come down from the mountains and hills are regulars.

Stray international tourists with back packs or small hire cars will occasionally chance upon the eatery or get the nod from a local.

You can order anything to eat as long at it is cooked in a large metal pot in advance.

Although the food won't be winning Michelin stars or have restaurant critics writhing around in wordy orgasmic ecstasy, the delicious grub will fill your stomach and won't leave a huge dent in your wallet.

Favourites with the clientele are proven homemade winners. Bolognese with finely diced rashers of smoked streaky bacon. Chilli combining freshly ground coffee, chocolate, brown sugar and imported dark ale. And a seafood and chicken paella made with fresh locally sourced clams, prawns and squid. For the vegetarians there is ratatouille, a succulent rich tomato dish with soft aubergine, courgette and peppers.

All the dishes are served with pasta or rice and as much garlic bread as you want.

You can wash the food down with a choice of local red and white wines from the vineyards in the mountains, carbonated water from underground reservoirs or lager or cider.

Spirits, especially Jack Daniels, are strictly no go. Just the smell of bad old Jack brings back all the nightmares.

The restaurant's chef and her assistant cook twice a week on Sundays and Wednesday, school and social commitments allowing. They play music, sing and dance around the tiny kitchen.

While they cook and chop, prepare and taste, four rescue Staffordshire Bull Terriers, two brindle, two sandy brown, guard their human pack leaders, large brown eyes tracking their every move, grateful for new lives, second chances after tough beginnings. The owner runs the restaurant on a shoestring.

More often than not, she'll jot down the orders and place the pad down the front of her tight black jeans. More for convenience's sake than any attempts at salaciousness. During the day, the sun warms generously without becoming an oven.

At night the most spectacular light show on earth takes place under a silver moon and a trillion stars.

Soft breezes from the Caribbean blow across the beach.

It's the sort of place you can spend your whole life dreaming about discovering and never find, unless, like one of the sandy coloured hounds, you're born Lucky.

The two girls siesta when the sun is at its highest, although Coni and Scarlett jokingly call it nest o'clock, in the upstairs apartment above their tiny secluded restaurant, a stone's throw from an equally secluded private beach off the beaten tourist track.

Before they open for the evening session, you can catch the duo on the beach by the ocean's edge. Scarlett, the blossoming assistant, is growing daily, exercising the free spirited hounds. Their tails wag madly as they gallop in ever widening circles, crashing through the waves. She screams out their names with delight as they dash here, there and everywhere with gay abandon. Alfie. Buckley. Lucky. And Sophie, named after a good friend.

Up ahead is Coni McHale, USA citizen, American Girl, the owner of Jak's Beach Hut, although calling it a hut is probably an exaggeration.

It's not really a hut, more of a shack.

Nothing to write home about, which is the way she likes it. Jak's is not forever but it will do until Scarlett's education takes precedence and they move to a city but not the one that occasionally sends shivers down her spine. The USA sounds mighty tempting.

Apparently she has relatives on her mother's side.

They live in Phoenix, Arizona and one day she will visit the Sunshine State.

She knows Scarlett will also spread her wings and fly from the nest with a new love in her life. When she does, she hopes she can find love too, that the delay will allow her to trust men and feel comfortable and safe within an intimate relationship.

She also knows one day, sooner or later, Scarlett will invariably ask about her father, whether he lives or is chasing stardust amongst the planets.

Of course, she'll lie to her daughter just the once, tell her they named the restaurant after him, and yes, he was a good man, their saviour, their White Stallion Man who soared High into the Sky to Rescue Them Both.

What was he like, she'll ask her mum and Coni will say he had the most amazing Ice Cold Blue Eyes you could imagine. Those gorgeous Ice Cold Blue Eyes had hidden depths of warmth behind them if he let you get close to him.

Naturally, the co-owner of Jak's Beach Hut and a small dog sanctuary in the mountains is in no rush for any of this to happen.

Time is not her master.

The clock does not torment her. Scarlett is not at risk, not in this tiny corner of paradise.

You'll see Coni on the beach, very tall for a woman, long black hair tied in a pony tail bouncing on her long, straight bronzed back, earphones and an iPod playing the songs she loves.

You'll have to be very fast and fit to catch her because she runs and she runs and runs and runs, happily.

.. away from the beach, the inevitable mind games over money...

189

In death's aftermath, there is money to be had. Lots of it. Life changing sums. But how far would you go to get your hands on it? What would you sacrifice? Your identity? Your name? Your reputation? Your sanity? The lives of three young shaven-headed homeless women washed up murdered on a seashore? Or even your own? Money changes everything but everyone has to pay a price.

Buy £8.99 at www.amazon.co.uk
Or direct at www.six10publishing.co.uk